UNEXPECTED GUESTS

at Blackbird Lodge

UNEXPECTED GUESTS

at Blackbird Lodge

—— a novel ——

Joyce Hicks

Unexpected Guests at Blackbird Lodge: a novel

For information about this title or to order other books and/or electronic media, contact the publisher:

Encore Books
joycebhicks.com

ISBNs:
978-0-578-35018-9 (print)
978-0-578-37188-7 (eBook)

Printed in the United States of America

Cover design: Melissa Washburn
Interior design: 1106 Design

Dedicated to those who have preserved the Adirondacks
Forever Wild

1

Required Reading

Still hot! Charlotte stared at the book jacket photo. Otis Teeter Staszcyk had turned into a more pronounceable and hip writer, O.T. Bookman—intense gaze, slicked-back dark hair, and five-o'clock shadow. Ducking behind a rack of magazines, Charlotte pressed his photo to her cheek. Their passion on the paisley couch in his faculty office was ancient history, but agreeable memories arose, nonetheless.

"Twenty-eight seventy-five, Ms. Adamsley."

She saw the shop owner was pulling together counter stools for their usual reader chat. "That guy, O.T. Bookman," he pointed to the hardback in her hand, "made quite a splash years ago."

"So I've heard. Thanks for ordering." She was about to run her credit card, then paid cash instead. "Got to run today."

"I bet you're busy with him coming to your place. Is he there yet?"

Ordinarily she would provide details.

"Next week." She called out as the door jangled shut.

Nineteen years ago, she had been a master of fine arts candidate in the writing program at Ann Arbor where Otis was a lecturer. Within days he would reappear in her life, the lead mentor for a writing retreat at Blackbird Lodge. This shocking turn of events forced her to break a vow never to read his prize-winning book and, what was more disquieting, to prepare her husband for a disclosure this guest could necessitate.

Charlotte felt her heart race and her vision field flatten as she drove the lodge van, the book riding on the console like a mortar. In a turnout, she rummaged the glove box but found nothing to tamp down the panic. *Maybe a good time to try meditation.* Eyes closed and hands folded, she whispered, "Inhale calm, exhale chaos." *Or was it "inhale chaos, exhale calm"? Or "om"? Inhale, slow exhale, inhale, exha—*

Resistance to reading the author bio was futile. After listing accolades, the text concluded with "O.T. Bookman teaches at Boston College. He and romance writer Luella Larkin and their daughter reside in Massachusetts."

Charlotte had googled him a time or two—well, lots of times—but having his book in hand under his new name was physical evidence of his life without her. She read the bio aloud, substituting her own name and embroidering embellishments. ". . . lives with their daughter, Alice, and his wife, Charlotte Louise Murphy, National Book Award author now at Harvard."

She closed her eyes to invite a scene. *Their Boston brownstone on Beacon Hill with an entrance hall of black-and-white tile. Stairs with a cherry bannister lead to the bedrooms and their study. Her desk overlooks the cloistered garden at the back; his overlooks the street. The paisley couch faces the fireplace. When Alice asks why they keep that raggedy thing, they just laugh—*HONK!

Weak after her panic attack, Charlotte had leaned on the horn. How she ended up driving this lodge van years ago was no mystery. Without a man, job, or book deal after finishing her MFA, she found a return home unthinkable, so she went to the vast Adirondack Park in northern New York for resort work. Mountains and physical labor had sounded restorative and real-life after stifling academic culture and romantic fiasco.

A mile from Blackbird Lodge, Charlotte stopped at the general store for coffee and collapsed at a table by the beer fridge. Flannel-clad loiterers reminded her of her early naivete about her move, how with "The People" she would write while learning to garden, make yogurt, or raise alpacas.

Something about the Midwest, maybe the bland quality of her middle-class life, imbued her with optimism that she deduced hadn't led to good storytelling. Only a handful of her pieces had been published. At twenty-four, she had been positive new geography and perspectives were essential in her quest to becoming a serious writer.

Sipping her coffee, Charlotte meditated over this decision nearly two decades old. That flyover-country optimism led her to think that after a year she would be chock-full of stories about colorful characters and would win a fellowship or teaching position somewhere.

As she flipped the pages of *Drowning in Freedom*, she leaned against the fridge, the rattling condenser reminding her of what needed repair at Blackbird Lodge. Too late she had discovered "real life" had a way of becoming your life. That happened after she met the striking and uncomplicated Will Adamsley, who lived the real life of the remote North, helping his parents run their aging resort. When a snowmobile accident killed them both, Will was in need of a wife. She had been available and in need of something too.

———— • ————

2

— SATURDAY —

Guest Book Entries

A WEEK LATER CHARLOTTE STOOD IN THE DRIVEWAY calling out goodbyes and muttering "at last" as she waved to the Douglass family, as their Volvos pulled out of Blackbird Lodge.

"But isn't it good to see them every year?"

Will's question felt like a reproach, and she waited for his yearly assessment.

"They're like family." He squeezed her shoulders, then headed for the disheveled lodge.

"More like the Kennedys, we being the poor relations." She watched him walk toward the kitchen door favoring his right knee that took a beating from the long days.

Year after year, the Douglass clan rented all the cabins for a week. She knew Blackbird needed the full-house income, but the Douglasses were the kind of dynastic family North Country people loved to hate. The Douglass children attended prep schools where they learned to sail and speak French, and the Douglass women played tennis all winter to keep their sculpted biceps and calves. North Country women got up before dawn for an icy commute, some going as far as Utica, and hoped the kids made the bus.

In minutes swiped during errands or late at night, Charlotte had found the time to read the four-hundred pages of *Drowning in Freedom* on top of serving as both upstairs maid and host for the Douglasses. At one point she had even floated in a canoe to get away from them. And O.T. Bookman's opus? It was great though she had planned to find it otherwise. Some passages brought her to tears or rage remembering where she had suggested an edit, the two of them working all night. And the plot was clever and insightful, with the language and pacing skillful, and in some passages, lyrical. She couldn't help but like it.

After just a few years at Blackbird Lodge, she saw the condescension and naivete in her initial motives for moving up north. The local people pretty much were like people everywhere except here they used a snowmobile to go to the sports bar in winter. The few women engaged in the arts of alpaca-raising, spinning, and canning saw her as an outsider. Homemade yogurt was just too homemade tasting, as if it were cultured in an old shoe. More disappointing, her writing faltered.

In the lodge after the Douglass send-off, Charlotte made a self-appraisal in the mirror over the buffet. *Have I aged a lot?* She didn't want an answer from Will. He would just tell her he loved her no matter what. *No matter what, what?*

The mirror led to no truth other than she'd better spritz the glass even though its haze was permanent. Early on she had used vinegar and newsprint in her determination to get through the silvery fog, feeling there must be something behind it as in *Through the Looking-Glass*, the story of their daughter's namesake. Charlotte's hair had been long and golden brown when she decided to stay inside the boundaries, called the Blue Line, of the Adirondack Park. Recently fearful of looking like the women who handed out oatmeal-flax gorp when kids expected chocolate cookies, she kept her hair shoulder length and got color touch-ups.

There were only twelve hours to recover from the week of Douglass lake fun and dining. Will said the Douglass family stays were reminiscent of what was common in the days when families stayed in the mountains for weeks at a time, bringing their dogs, horses, and servants with them. She watched Will through the open dining room door whistling while making piecrusts. She loved his hands, a reminder of his initial appeal, his skill in culinary and mechanical arts. His competence where previous boyfriends, especially Otis, fumbled, as well as his availability, had awakened her Midwestern practicality. He was robust and handsome, and after his parents' accident, properted and emotionally needy. He had fit the bill for a father for an Ann Arbor pregnancy.

Still brooding about the Douglasses, Charlotte went into the kitchen. "Did you notice the garnet pendant on Tabby?" She put her arms around Will to lean her forehead against his back. "I bet that's from a 'honey-I-made-a-boo-boo' truce with her husband. Seems like she'd be afraid of losing it, catching it on a branch or something."

"Tabby? Can't say as I did." He fluted a crust with unusual concentration. "Probably a birthday gift, don't you think?"

That was Will all over. The Douglass clan could do no wrong.

Charlotte stepped outside to spare him an acid comment. It never bothered him how the guests prospered while they were barely making it. *I'm not supposed to mind either,* she thought, twisting her wedding band that still lacked a diamond.

After all, she had chosen to stay up here in the North, unlike Will who was born into the Adamsleys, a family more long-standing than the Douglasses. Dating back to the nineteenth century, the unsmiling photos of Will's branch of the family hung in the hall. The women wore dark dresses, and Charlotte suspected one baby photo was a postmortem pose. The original Adamsleys had been awarded land parcels in the steep valleys of Massachusetts and New York for their service in the Continental Army during the American Revolution. Will's reclusive branch of the family had eventually relocated farther north for farming in this obscure region. By the end of the nineteenth century, their livelihood relied, Will had explained, on the summer camps of the wealthy. Through an oddity, Blackbird Lodge fell to the Adamsleys in the 1930s. Charlotte had been able to piece together little of the full history. Surely there were many stories there.

Charlotte went around to the front porch to arrange the hickory chairs and tables into an iconic lodge tableau. She would show O.T. Bookman that he wasn't the only one with success. She had a kingdom, a three-story lodge and eight cabins set on a hundred acres. *And Alice!*

Fashioned after a Swiss chalet, the lodge was built as a retreat from New York City, but when the mountains became less fashionable, Blackbird had been rented as a sanitorium. Village women had also taken in people suffering from tuberculosis despite the danger of transmission. *Thank God I missed that era,* Charlotte thought while she pulled loose bark from a birch card table. Cleaning the rooms of healthy people could be disgusting enough. Satisfied the porch looked like a period stage set, she began a walk-through of the cabins before the cleaning help arrived.

Each cabin had a guest book, a resort tradition Will insisted they maintain. Sometimes the entries raised Charlotte's morale and helped in estimating who might return next year. She began a review of the Douglass week.

In precise penmanship, the entry in Bluebird cabin's guest book read, "Had a great time as always. No mosquitoes inside this summer. Thanks for fixing the screen. Raymond said he found the Thursday roast beef kind of tough, not like last year. The new lemon bars were delicious."

Leave it to the senior Douglasses to complain in the book rather than talk with them. Charlotte was about to rip out the page, but no, Lucille would be sure to look through the book next year. The roast beef and lemon bar details Charlotte would pass along to Will.

Tabby and her husband had stayed in the one-bedroom Whippoorwill cabin since they had no kids. They had already rebooked, but Charlotte scanned anyway for Tabby's entry.

"I guess it will always be Auld Lang Syne for me at Blackbird. Loved the comfort food, Will, served just right, as usual."

"Comfort food?" Charlotte said. This Douglass entry might spur him to update, but the song reference was a puzzle. *Maybe Will will get it.*

The Cardinal cabin maxed the sleeping combinations with a queen bed in one bedroom, twin beds in a shallow loft, and a daybed under the windows in the living room. It looked ready for the cleaning crew, so Charlotte opened the guest book. The handwriting here was irregular, that of a writer used to keyboards.

"Blackbird Lodge has a way of bringing families together. Thanks so much, Charlotte and Will, for making it happen every year. Our fourteen-year-old even forgot how awful we are!"

A smiley face was drawn at the end. *Lucky you*, Charlotte thought. The stressed-looking woman had thanked her profusely for a minor change in a box lunch for this daughter whose expression of resignation faded only slightly over the week.

It was a look Charlotte and Will had come to know well. After only a few weeks at college, their daughter Alice evaluated them as hopelessly misogynistic. Will had looked the word up to figure out how to regain his "cool dad" status. As the year went on, Alice's conversation was peppered with polemics about racial and gender inequality, gender fluidity, privilege, and preferred pronouns.

Charlotte put down the guest book to stare at the empty dock where Alice and her childhood friends used to spend summer days. This summer she often took off for Albany, and today the parking spot for her Honda was empty. Charlotte sighed over yesterday's mother-daughter miscue. Backpack in hand, Alice had announced that Chris was threatening suicide after a breakup via a text.

"Sounds like she needs a friend," Charlotte had offered.

"'*They*' mom," Alice had yelled as her car door slammed.

Charlotte closed Cardinal's guest book. Perhaps next year the Douglass woman would be writing about gender fluidity.

The other entries had been complimentary and sentimental—the beautiful lake, the good times, warm days, cool nights, and so forth. The entries showed the Douglass week had been a success. They would all come back. The book from Cardinal was full—it had been there five years—so she took it to the lodge library.

On a whim, she pulled out the books from the year of her own first night at Blackbird as Will's guest. If she had made an entry, it would be in Whip-poor-will, where Will had snuck in after lights-out in the lodge. Yes, October 15, there was her entry.

Her handwriting was so self-consciously stylish. She must have thought Will's mother might look at it.

"I already love it here, my first night."

Is this love holding up? she wondered. She closed the book before her thoughts wandered.

———— • ————

3

Party Time at Rosco's

AFTER SANDWICHES AT THE KITCHEN TABLE, Charlotte went to her desk in what had been the servants' quarters. Just as she was opening a file of notes on her laptop, a reminder pinged: "Go to party at Rosco's." She closed the laptop, the story idea that had been skittering in her thoughts evaporating.

Rosco's, a short drive from the lodge, had a peeling log exterior that discouraged tourists. The tavern was primarily a place for complaining about the government in Albany while watching hockey in the winter. The current owner had tried to rename the bar Rinkside Seats when he added large flat-screens, but the old name stuck, though Rosco had been in Florida ten years.

As she and Will got out of their jeep, Charlotte said, "Let's not stay too long."

Will opened the bar door, letting out a waft of beer-scented air and the guitar riff of "Satisfaction."

"Must be classic rock night," he said and added, "Gossip with the girls, Char. That's all you have to do."

She felt his arm propel them forward. "It can't be that hard," he added, just as he had oftentimes over the years.

He couldn't see how the women treated her like an outsider. The articles and stories she wrote for magazines only compounded her difference from them. They still regarded her as not grounded in the North and thus suspect. Charlotte sighed. *Maybe they were right.*

Balloons signaled the party area, as did the pitchers of margaritas. Charlotte wedged into a seat next to Kate, a county librarian. Kate handed her a filled glass. Talk of the junior summer soccer and baseball leagues swirled about them. Charlotte drifted. She was proud of Alice's success with her freshman year at the University at Albany and listened for an opening to talk. She felt Kate shake her arm.

"All ready for your writer guests?" Kate shouted over the music. "Do you think there'll be a public reading?"

The Yankees' home run brought a roar from the bar. "What?" Charlotte leaned toward Kate.

"A reading! The famous writer, O.T. Bookman." Kate topped off their drinks. "You told me all about the retreat."

Charlotte nodded as Kate congratulated her again at securing "the big bucks" week, but her friend's enthusiasm made her uneasy. Exactly what had she said or implied to Kate about the participants?

"Yeah, O.T. Bookman. I'm sure he'll be fascinating!" Charlotte shouted upsetting her glass in an effort to gesture casually.

Kate mopped up. "That other writer, the memoirist, won a book prize last year, Lydia Beauvais Galesberg." She leaned in close to say the full name in Charlotte's ear. "With a name like that, she'd have to be a writer. You must be over the moon, Charlotte. And a New York editor coming too."

Kate delivered a high five, but Charlotte's hand was limp.

She made a shoulders-to-ears indication of excitement and shoved her chair back. "The editor's only here a couple of days. I'll let you know about a reading. Right now, I've got loose ends—" A wad of napkins fell as she stood up, but she left them and went outside.

"I've got to get a grip," she told herself as she walked around the parking lot. Of course, her sanguine attitude with Kate was a lie. The retreat inquiry and subsequent signed contract was the lodge's best business news of the year, let alone having a New York editor on the premises for two days. The complete roster listing the writing mentors had been another sort of news and arrived only two weeks ago. She had brooded over how much to tell Will.

As she circled the picnic tables under the spruces, a branch sharply tugged her hair, as if Nature were giving her a sign. Perhaps Bookman's arrival was castigation for her perplexing unrest. Or an atonement opportunity for sins of commission and omission? Or for simple idiocy? Maybe all of the above.

We could have survived without the check. But rising taxes, outstanding bills, college tuition—the list went on and couldn't be batted away like the spruce branch. It was too late to cancel these people, too late to reason with Will, too late to do anything except carry on. After a final tromp around the picnic tables, she went back inside.

———— • ————

4

Elsewhere

Saturday evening in his Boston brownstone, O.T. Bookman threw jeans, boxers, and socks in a canvas bag, the kind favored at Ivy League schools. His position at Boston College was close enough, at least geographically. He went into the bathroom for toiletries, pausing over his razor. Without Luella to complain, he just might start a beard during the workshop. He rubbed his jaw, which now had the manly five-o'clock shadow seen on guys with portfolios or shovels.

"Mirror, mirror on the wall, who's . . . ," he muttered while assessing his hair for thickness. All was well there for the boyish look he cultivated. Moving on to his blue eyes and smile lines, O.T. thought to himself, *I'm only in my late forties after all. DiCaprio and Pitt are still leading men well into their forties and fifties.*

O.T. ransacked his closet for shirts and outerwear for the unpredictable Adirondack weather. Should he bring his cashmere sweater, the one described by a redheaded coed as "Caribbean blue like your eyes"? He stuffed the potential talisman under the jeans when he heard Luella coming to exert approval in packing.

"I found my famous writer jacket." He held up the limp corduroy sports coat dating back to his readings at bookstores as an unknown. The leather elbow patches and sprinkle of burn holes stood as proof of his writer identity.

"You better bring the shirt your seminar students gave you." Luella folded it so the imprint "Will Write for Money" would not crease in the suitcase.

He kissed her, trying for a slow one, but she broke away. "Maddie's got another cold." She went into the bedroom alcove where their toddler slept. O.T. found her leaning over the crib listening to the child's breathing. "Wish you were going to be here to help me."

Luella in a shorty nightie bending over their daughter tugged at his heart, not just his groin. She was a perfect mother, playful and patient. By "help," he knew she meant get up with her while she changed diapers and rocked Maddie. He would be allowed to fetch things and check online whether the child was old enough for cold meds. Had he gotten up at night for his boys? Probably not often enough. "Do it right this time" was a mantra he tried to keep to, but a week without Luella and their daughter would be, well, rejuvenating.

He hastily arranged his face into an expression of regret. At the retreat he would be on his game—mesmerizing audiences with his readings, enlightening listeners through soliloquies on style, and signing autographs reminiscent of his months on the *New York Times* best-seller list. However, at Blackbird Lodge there would be no pretty coeds hanging around the refreshment table and monitoring stacks of his books. One graduate assistant was coming, one very willing to take on all the work of the retreat, but it wouldn't be like the old days. *Nothing was.* He snapped back into the long silence where he could feel Luella's worry.

"I'm sure Maddie will be fine," he said, then softened his remark by stroking the child's head. The little girl was the apple of his eye, a trite expression he now understood perfectly.

"I still don't see why you have to go away. Why can't you write in your study here?"

He dithered with the crib toys looking for an answer. Luella could write at her desk, a coffee shop, or the car, churning out competent pages. "Christian bodice rippers," as he called her novels in private. "Historical romances for faith readers" noted the little emblem on the covers that drew a growing fan base. Negotiations were underway for foreign-language editions.

"We need the money." That was an easy answer, easier than the ones about getting back in the game or keeping ahead of her.

"How much are you getting?"

"Three thousand bucks and a week in the woods for writing."

"At least it's a senior retreat this time, O.T." She patted down his suitcase like a TSA agent and pulled the zipper.

Was this a reference to that other retreat and the suggestive text messages from that poet? O.T. wondered again if Luella had read them, then grimaced over the reminder of these writers being senior citizens. He would be holed up at a mountain resort with a dozen in their dotage who had probably signed up after flipping a coin. Heads, china painting; tails, writing.

"Oh, yes, each one will be penning a memoir on the virtues of life in prewar or postwar America."

"Which war?" Luella said as she checked the label on the nighttime cold medicine.

He resisted comment. "Or maybe something about enriching rural life like beheading chickens and Aunt Ina's bean recipe. Or maybe an immigrant experience, Statue of Liberty, Ellis Island, beheading chickens, the whole shebang." His pantomime brought Luella to giggles.

"You're terrible!" She kissed him lightly. "You old people have lots of fascinating stories."

"Yeah, I should write a book." References to their age difference made her laugh and him amorous.

His goodbye lovemaking was delayed for a few minutes more while he packed a folder from his desk drawer, pages he had fussed over for years. The novel had moved across half a dozen generations of technology and now resided in the cloud. He hoped he could recall where and the password.

Why can't I finish the damn thing? The question surfaced for the millionth time.

The bracing Adirondack air, the quiet lake, sympathetic golden-agers who would admire him and give him plenty of solitude to write—maybe this time would be it. And his old New York friend Zenobia Daly would be there at the end of the week, now with her own publishing house. *Won't that be interesting?*

In a fourth-floor walk-up in Boston, Cinny, graduate student in speculative fiction, ABD (all but dissertation)—a young adult dystopian series, incomplete—filled her backpack with chargers and her electric boyfriend, though if she played her cards right . . .

At yesterday's coffee break, she and Mina had evaluated O.T. as fling material. He was kind of old for a hookup—"like doing it with my tax accountant," Cinny had said—but he had old-fashioned sex appeal nonetheless. She recalled their conversation.

"Luella Larkin is a lot younger than him. Do you think he's a pleaser?" Cinny leaned toward Mina.

"In my experience older men are not in such a hurry." Mina fiddled with her vape. "They care more about what a woman wants."

Mina had expelled a cloud of cotton candy–scented vapor with this tidbit from her extensive campus dalliances. She had even romanced the rail-thin adjunct in physics, the one with unintelligible English, Cinny had heard.

Cinny wondered if O.T. would care about what she wanted. *Perhaps time will tell.* She knew he found her attractive. He ordered sandwiches so he could help her until midnight with department grant applications, chummily adding keystrokes over her shoulders. Other times, he talked to her for hours about his latest book, then gave her handwritten pages to enter into the manuscript. "To give you more editing insights," he'd say. His offer of the paid position of assistant in the workshop wasn't a surprise. She had shown herself to be smart and efficient. To prepare for the week she had gone through another hair iteration, maybe a little eccentric this time, with one side straight and the other bouncy curls. Mina declared the look inventive.

Enough speculation about the hookup potential, Cinny upbraided herself. *I ought to review notes.* O.T. depended on her to run this workshop and make him look good. And she would. And then he would owe her big time, leaving no way he could escape taking her novel draft seriously. She really needed his help. Not just his vacant nodding when she talked about the dystopia she had created. He ought to introduce her to a skilled content editor, someone who could get her out of the bog in the middle of the book. How many nights had she spent with her plot in the quicksand, each grabbed root a false handhold? She gazed at the shelf of books she yearned to emulate with plots so depressing only teens would want to keep reading. Several were written by women about her age.

She took up her retreat outline, and clicking her pen, she started marking up the page with arrows, carets, and strike-throughs. O.T. had said, "Don't bother me with details." And she hadn't. After three years in grad school, she knew the drill for a workshop: guided writing, encouragement, gentle criticism, and performance. Her hour-by-hour outline would make them a highly professional team.

There were two wild cards she couldn't anticipate completely. There was the editor, Zenobia Daly, who would be coming from New York and a secondary writer guest from the University of Iowa, a team member but not a leader. Why a university in the middle of nowhere like Iowa should be such a mecca for fiction, Cinny couldn't fathom. Her rejected application still rankled. In any case, she hadn't bothered to read the woman's book yet since she wasn't famous like O.T. Cinny looked at his photo on his last book, published several years ago, comparing it to the brochure photo. *Yeah, airbrushed.* Not that he was exactly sought after these days, although his Google search results still glowed with earlier awards and reviews.

But in a secret drawer he had a terrific manuscript that he had shown her last week. He was holding the book for the right time and was working on getting the last chapters perfect. Something that would "touch a chord in our times," he had said, though it must touch a lot of times since he had been working on the book for more than a decade. Why, she was only in ninth grade when he was writing the first chapters.

Cinny's thoughts rambled along as she searched her meager wardrobe for items that would be workshop appropriate yet fun and sexy in a mountain lodge. At the bottom of the closet she found two candidates, a university logo shirt and another one with a feminist activism logo, a nonoffensive one, however. A lace camisole and cleavage-showing silk top and slim black pants were needed for going out, if there was an opportunity. *Or for late nights by the fire.*

Whatever else went on, her job was to make O.T. shine and give him hours away from the writers so that he could finish those last chapters and impress the New York editor. He had an agent, of course, but he'd said that he might market this manuscript to a press himself.

What luck! She would be right there beside him to show the New York editor her own manuscript. She tossed a fresh copy into her suitcase, just the first of a four-part series she had sketched out.

🙠

In a subdivision in Iowa, Dr. Lydia Beauvais Galesberg packed her suitcase with black leggings, an oversized pearl gray sweater, two shirts, workout togs, a turquoise-and-purple Italian tunic, jewelry, and her jacket and hiking boots. She had found that these writing gigs went better if she played her expected part: warmly eccentric memoirist. Colleagues often said she looked like a student, her ash-blond hair in an elaborate French braid and her figure rich in curves. With her sons out of the house, one in a paid internship and the other in an entry-level position, she was discovering the pleasure of taking time for her appearance and body. She threw in some lace underthings and nightwear. Generally, one never knew whom one might meet at these things.

This time she did know.

"My ex." She spoke to a strappy silver nightgown.

He was the lead writer. Otis Teeter Bookman, boy wonder, first novel a best seller at twenty-seven, limp follow-ups, and then, nothing. The world was still waiting! They had divorced shortly before he changed his name and the first book came out, leaving her with two boys, a then-unfinished PhD, and no job.

Her phone rang. She looked at the caller ID. "Mother, of course."

"Why should you give that narcissistic jerk the time of day, after the way he treated you?" The call began without a preamble.

Her mother must have learned the details of the workshop in a senior education catalog because Lydia would not have told her that O.T. was one of the writers in residence.

"Lydia, honey, are you sure this will be good for you?" Her voice oozed concern.

"Mother, we divorced years ago." Lydia laid a photo book of her sons in the suitcase. Older people had photos of their grandchildren to pass around, and she would like to have snapshots to show off too.

"You don't want to go into a depression. You just tell the event people you have the grippe. I can hear from your voice you have a bug already. You could stay with me and work along on that book of yours."

After her mother referred to her current manuscript as if it were a craft project, Lydia went on the defensive, abandoning her therapist's advice about treating her mother like a neighbor. "I do not have a bug."

"Now listen, dear, let me give you some advice about Otis."

"Mom—"

"No, you listen to me. He's just like your father. You know how they say daughters marry someone like their father, which you did absolutely, even though I could see the resemblance and told you so."

Lydia opened drawers at random in the kitchen. She wasn't at all sure that O.T. had been like her father other than the divorce part. O.T. was passionate, either high or low. He either loved or hated whatever he was doing. He was easy to get along with or impossible, one of the reasons the boys had always found him a difficult father. Her dad had been so secretive that they never knew he had a woman and child where he went on business until he finally decided to settle there. O.T. also had fooled around, but he had been so bad at hiding liaisons that it came as no surprise when he decided he wanted out. And she did too.

"So, what I'm saying is, you should not, I emphasize *not*, get involved with him again, even for the week."

Nesting the spoons together in the silverware compartment, Lydia decided her mother's advice sealed an idea she had been playing with. Yes, if O.T. made a romantic move, she would agree, or perhaps offer one herself. Why not? She was an independent woman now. Sex was one thing they had done well together.

"I just know you're thinking about him."

Lydia pictured her mother as a neighbor. "Thanks so much for the advice. I will really think over what you have said. Have a nice week. Bye."

The thing about her mother's advice was that it was sound. This was always the problem with family. She packed her manuscript, a memoir about life with a boy-wonder novelist. She just wasn't sure about the final chapters yet.

✒

In other bedrooms that Saturday evening, writers packed for the writing week. Most packed their dreams carefully alongside their sweaters, notes, chapbooks, novellas, or laptops. Only those who signed up primarily to escape an empty house packed just a new notebook or tablet. The others hoped that in the right atmosphere, among the right advice and the right vibes, or even in the competition-charged air of talent, that creativity and good luck would smile on their efforts.

They hoped to enter the zone, that fabled place where the writer watched as characters spoke and acted on their own, where the author was only a conduit, the laptop an electronic Ouija board directed from the Other Side. That place the Great Ones found—J. K. Rowling, Sandra Cisneros, Stephen King, Toni Morrison, or even Dickens, all those who kept going until they received recognition.

Some of the workshop writers hoped for publication, the graduation of an infant idea that filled a notebook. Others hoped to write away pain or defeat. Some looked for release through words, a cathartic spewing about a cancer, a wayward husband, or an aged parent. A text might be thankful praise to God for the beauty of nature, for time spent together, for a new grandchild, for a remission, for winning the lottery. Rabbits, rigor mortis, robbers, retribution, righteous indignation, reclamation, and reconciliation filled the notebooks they brought along.

Some writers would come or leave empty-handed. The mentors would tour them through some exercises, just as a guide had taken them through St. Mark's Basilica or down the Colorado River. They hoped for a good time, even a hoot. That was all.

However, most attendees felt or had told friends: "If I only had had the time . . . If I had gotten in the mood . . . If

I had started younger . . ." Each could have written a book. Each had a favorite title to mention followed by "I could have written that." So, suitcases and shoulder bags and laptops were weighted down with hopes, as well as pajamas, as, from various places, people readied for Blackbird Lodge.

———·———

5

— SUNDAY —

Swiss Steak

THERE WAS AN HOUR AND A HALF LEFT before Charlotte's drive to Old Forge where she would pick up the guests arriving via bus transport or their own cars. This Sunday morning, she and Will drank coffee on the porch while he did the crossword puzzle, but she couldn't focus on the clues he read aloud.

"Sometime," Charlotte spoke as if an idea had just come casually to mind, "we're going to have to explain more to Alice."

"About?" Will tried to erase an answer but the newsprint tore.

"You can't keep pretending there's nothing to talk to her about." The tension she was feeling seeped into her voice.

"At least you didn't say 'real dad'!" Will used air quotes and then pulled her onto his lap. "She's always known about how she has no genetic relationship to me. She and I aren't interested in the details."

"We really should, no, I really should tell . . ." But no words would come. Maybe more wasn't necessary because maybe O.T. wouldn't remember her at all. *Why should he?*

Will shrugged. "Yeah, I agree. Why are you thinking of this now, Char?"

She stood up tripping on the rocker of his heavy Adirondack chair. "I don't know. All the trips to Albany, her new friends. Alice just seems unsettled."

"Is that the word for it?" Will put down the crossword page. "That's one clue that's not in my puzzle. I'll think about talking with her sometime. Soon. I agree with you. Honesty is the best policy."

With that aphorism, Charlotte's heart began the hiccupped beats she'd noticed lately, so she dry swallowed a pill from her pocket. No point in telling Will about the symptoms because their cause was clear to her. If she could afford a therapist, she might have had a Klonopin handy instead of an aspirin.

"Go for a nice swim, honey, while you have a chance. Don't you worry about the writing people or Alice. She's fine." He squeezed her waist as she passed him. "We'll make sure the folks have a good time. You'll charm the socks off those professors."

Will was right. Sometimes exercise killed worry, so she went to the boathouse for an old bathing suit. But in the cold lake her quickened pulse reanimated her hours in O.T.'s office. The monastic third-floor setting in a house for faculty offices had belied his lifestyle. The saggy paisley couch oozing English Leather and mildew had been a passion pit, if Charlotte were to name it now. He had often read aloud from his scrawled manuscript pages as they embraced.

"You are my little duck." She could still feel him cupping her chin with his narrow, writerly fingers. Oh, she had been such an idiot thinking they would publish together, or travel, or whatever—each the other's muse.

She swam along to an inlet, skirting the water lilies that caught her legs. In the shallows fallen branches were enmeshed, like the lilies, beautiful but hazardous to a weak swimmer who might find the bottom give way. Today they struck her as emblematic of how the present only layered over the past. A false step could cause drowning. She returned to their beach and rearranged a kayak and canoe before climbing the steps to the lodge.

In their bedroom Will was waiting. "Time for a quick one?" His hand along her thigh felt good as she stepped out of her suit.

"Can't. I'm already late."

"Whatever happened to the nooner?" He patted a place for her on the bed.

"A teenager, full cabins, and three-course dinners," she said leaving out other reasons. Sometimes his moves were workman-like, and her own attention was unfocused too. There was blame to share.

"Maybe tonight if we can get the writing folks settled in?" He kissed her neck as he left the room. *Maybe.*

About to pull on her loose outdoorsy pants and lodge logo shirt, she stopped. Local festivals and outfitter catalogs made for little wardrobe variety. She paired combinations for their messages: the lodge help, outdoorswoman, soccer mom, quirky gal. She sighed. None said "successful, fulfilled, and sexy woman."

She scouted the closet again and found a midi, tie-dye dress. *Retro chic?*

The lavender cotton felt like gossamer falling over her hips and breasts. The last time she wore the dress Alice had been scornful. "Mom, is that Woodstock déjà vu? Get some regular clothes." But any daughterly interest was prized these days. Charlotte checked the mirror and added silver and turquoise bracelets to hide that they were hard up, she being not only innkeeper, host, and server but also van driver today.

She stopped by the kitchen, moving fast to discourage focus on the dress. "I'm on my way, Will. Mmm, smells good." *I owe him something.* She kissed his neck.

"It's Swiss steak." Tomato sauce was simmering, and he was chopping the onions with a dangerous chit-chit-chit motion as she shut the screen door.

Swiss steak, it must be Sunday. She resisted making the observation aloud. Her idea that they revamp the family-style, single-entrée offering always set off an argument.

After all these years, do you still not understand the family camp concept?

But other family resorts do well even with the expense of menu options.

Yes, and turned over ownership several times too!

Of course, I don't want that, I was only suggesting—

Perhaps he was getting somewhat stodgy, as her mother had warned her about marrying a man five years older. She shrugged off her irritation. How could she find fault with this good husband? Maybe the basil accent would disguise the pedestrian, low-cost nature of the main course.

Old Forge was a half-hour's drive over smooth tarmac climbing and falling through the woods. Taking the curves, windows open, was pure pleasure. These were not the friendly forests of her Michigan childhood vacations where third- and fourth-growth pines, oaks, and birches let in light, sandy lakes invited swimming, and even Lake Michigan warmed somewhat. But after a few seasons, Charlotte had adapted to the North Woods where the tall spruces and balsams cut the light. Other trees, surviving the harsh winters and earlier acid rain, stood bracken-covered and protective of the Adirondack Park. These woods attracted hikers willing to cross rocks and bogs to reach remote lakes. Part of her route followed a river with boulders and rapids at the wide curves. Though beautiful, today the scenery increased her unease. When her phone rang, she used speaker mode since the van had no Bluetooth.

"Mom?"

"Hi, honey." She and Alice could often have a congenial phone exchange, without the tension of being face-to-face.

"I'm coming home tonight and bringing Roy."

"Roy? Sure, you can bring home anyone." Charlotte's spirits rose tentatively.

"Don't get the idea this is a boyfriend, or something like that."

"What? No, of course not."

"Oh, BTW, Roy identifies as they."

Charlotte was glad Alice couldn't see her expression. Yes, she'd been told how pronouns were gender limiting. Will probably couldn't handle the grammatical gymnastics required, even for Alice, but she would try to.

"Tell Dad that, okay? The last time a guy came Dad got all weird." *That was because he had disgusting holes in his ears.* Charlotte refrained from comment.

"The lodge is full, but he can have the sleeping porch off the kitchen." Charlotte gave the van some gas on the curve.

"This is what I mean by weird. They can just use the other bunk in my room. What d'ya think?"

What she was thinking was, why couldn't Alice bring home a normal-looking boy, a boy using he/him/his pronouns and without holes in his ears? *A boy like the Douglass youth,* she finally admitted silently. Charlotte longed to find telltale signs of romance—flushed face, ill-adjusted shirt, even a rumpled bed in an empty cabin, anything that would say that this woke thing was a phase.

"Mom? It's okay, right?

"Sure, honey. Bring friends, ah, people, anytime."

"I'll get there to help with dinner. Love you, Mom."

Oh, yes, love. She and Will loved Alice more than the whole world, or each other, probably. She would assist in making Roy feel welcome, anything for Alice. Anything. Too late she thought how Alice being out of sight in Albany would have been better.

Rounding the last curve, Charlotte entered an organized hamlet, the look of prosperity welcome after the crossroad businesses nearer the lodge. Old Forge was the first resort community on the way north into the Adirondack Park from the Thruway exit at Utica and a refueling spot on the way out. The pleasure of talking to Alice was now replaced by panic. She parked at a distance from the meeting point to survey the people gathered. With their ice cream cones and excessive luggage, the people on the sidewalk were clearly the senior writers.

So, where's Mr. Best Seller? She tried out sarcasm to dampen her agitation.

The van engine cooled, contributing to the suspense by ticking irregularly. She flipped down the visor and leaned into the windshield for a better look while she rehearsed options for First Encounter.

Professional. *"Welcome. We're so pleased to host the work-shop at Blackbird."*

Blasé agreement to a previous acquaintanceship. *"Oh, of course, now I remember. We did meet at grad school."*

Amusement over the old days. *"We were all crazy young back then, right?"*

But her cool changed to heat when she saw the parked Lexus. There was Otis, now O.T., leaning on the hood, a hint of the handsome, dissolute bon vivant in his stance, gesturing with—*Is that an e-cigarette?*

But above all, he was still magnetic.

The lodge van door closed more loudly than Charlotte intended, but no one noticed her. The writers' voices were animated and loud.

"Loved your books."

"So nice of you to take us on."

"Brought all my poems."

At each offering, the man's smile was charismatic, warm, and sincere. *God, he hasn't changed a bit.* Charlotte felt transfixed by this stage set.

O.T. Bookman might be a fading star in the world of fiction, but he had been a supernova in her galaxy once. And how the nights had twinkled on the office couch when she had thought staying until midnight was justified. They were talking and writing, which made her overlook the tiny fact of his wife and family while they worked on his masterpiece. Why her moral compass had been so skewed became clear as she watched him, plausible but inexcusable, of course.

Was Alice doing something like that all those nights spent on campus? The question sprang on Charlotte. She and Will would be outraged about a violation of trust in the student-teacher covenant.

No one had looked Charlotte's way yet when a Mustang convertible pulled up. A woman waved jauntily, and Charlotte saw that O.T. was clearly surprised at her arrival. He stepped back as the woman, presumably Dr. Galesberg, offered her hand then made her way around the group, shaking all hands and chatting.

Next, gravel spewed from under the Lexus. O.T. had left the lot! The writers stared but turned away to lavish attention on the newer arrival.

The Blackbird Lodge welcome couldn't be delayed much longer. Charlotte approached a very young woman with a clipboard. "You must be Cynthia. At Blackbird we're all looking forward to the writers so much."

"Call me Cinny. I'll go over details with ya in a few minutes, okay? Two couples canceled yesterday, by the way, but after the money back deadline."

The girl-woman held out a hand attached to a fully tattooed arm. The roses had muted red buds entwined in thorny vines and leaves. Charlotte repressed a grimace as she took the offered hand. Alice hadn't gotten any body art at college, or not as far as she could see. She tore her eyes from the tattoo sleeve.

"I'll drive over closer," Charlotte said and dashed toward the van.

She hadn't really expected the reunion with Otis to be like a couple running across a field of daisies. She would step aside anyway, considering Will and Alice. But there should have been something, not his just getting in his car and not even seeing her—*or did he see me?*—and then her being bossed around by Thorn Rose.

This whole retreat would be a very complicated week.

———— · ————

6

First Impressions

Everyone says that you can't judge a book by its cover, but you surely might decide which one looks promising. Right away the writers sized up each other, their mentors, the graduate student assistant, their hosts, and the lodge to decide on the likelihood for creative vibes that week.

As the van pulled up outside Blackbird, Sarah, who was not supposed to be brooding about her recently deceased husband, thought of calling him to say how much he would love the rustic setting.

Westley made a withering appraisal of the lodge. The three-story building had a great chimney. The roofs overhung the eaves, and a deep porch overlooked the lake. A slight air of faded grace hung over the property. The lodge, its boathouse, and cottages had been built for the wealthy to maintain, but if one looked closely, the camp now struggled. A tiny side porch askew, mismatched shingles, and replaced fieldstones in a foundation took Westley's attention, and he made notes on a pocket tablet.

"Undeserving bastards," he muttered while watching Will welcome the ladies.

Millicent's first thought was about her new wardrobe as she took in the lodge. Rustic had not looked so forbidding in the outfitter catalog. The pinstripe red-and-white top and white capris should be saved for Florida. To cut costs, she had chosen to share a cabin, and her roomie seemed companionable enough, though she was a recent widow. Millicent hoped there would be no scenes. Some widows were downright tiresome, something she herself had carefully avoided. In fact, when she found Ralph dead in his chair with a church hymnal, she had felt relief. It wasn't that she didn't love him or wouldn't miss him. His censorious attitudes had begun to get to her, and with his heart failing, she knew she would not be the kind of helpmeet an invalid deserved, nor would he be the kind of invalid a good wife deserved. So, his death was a reprieve, both escaping a decline that might have shown their true colors. Her cabin roomie, Sarah, might have had quite a different experience.

Ruth helped Bea out of the van. Once a few yards into the property, the friends shrieked with delight.

"Bea, look, it's like a Santa's village," Ruth said as they took in the woodsy cabins that were scattered along the hill overlooking the lake.

"Oh, I'm sure we can write a good story here!" Bea said, thankful she had not insisted that her husband be her retreat companion. The nearest Cracker Barrel was back off the Thruway.

Westley rolled his eyes as he stood behind the women. Their conversation oozed with "darling" and "cozy" for the clapboard cabins, additions from a later era, that made him think of miniature golf. The prospect of meeting any decent writers here looked dim.

☙

Cinny had turned the group over to the innkeeper as soon as possible and now stood behind a tree to phone Mina. Since

O.T. had chosen to disappear, she needed ideas for defusing the catastrophe she had inadvertently orchestrated.

"How was I supposed to know Lydia was O.T.'s ex?" Cinny vented, and Mina sympathized.

Cinny outlined how O.T. had told her to pick out a writer from among the applicants.

"Had any included in their vita 'former wife of O.T. Bookman'? How was I supposed to know that the memoirist from Iowa was the former *Mrs.?*" She pronounced the title with distaste.

Mina agreed that after this screwup, O.T. probably wouldn't be willing to look at her manuscript the way he had promised.

☙

While the writers were settling in at the lodge and Cinny was working on her disaster management plan, O.T. was sipping a scotch. He had left the parking lot in Old Forge in search of a roadhouse and found Rosco's. *A place for a man to decompress*, he had thought to himself as he pulled into the gravel parking lot. Inside he replayed the scene that was too unbelievable for fiction.

When Lydia got out of the Mustang, he'd thought, *She's on time for once.* Then, *My God, that's Lydia!* Past and present collided. Until his timeline recalibrated, he'd had to lean on his car. Then what's-her-name, Celine, no, Cynthia had said in front of everyone, "This is Dr. Lydia Beauvais Galesberg. Dr. Bookman, have you met her before?"

He'd stumbled through saying they were well acquainted while Lydia looked like the Cheshire Cat. Only the most unintuitive person wouldn't guess a former relationship.

She was looking very good! Something about her, a new style? He continued to review the scene until his glass was empty, but he couldn't have another without looking like a lush. After texting Luella that he'd arrived, he headed to Blackbird with dread and anticipation for companions.

✎

With O.T. en route and the rest of the guests taking in the lodge, Will hustled suitcases and their owners into the cabins. Charlotte lingered, wondering what possessed her to wear the tie-dye dress. The guests were wearing what they felt was mountain lodge appropriate, as she should have too. Her showboating wardrobe was downright dumb. She was a grown woman, a land-rich one at that, and other than the kitchen, in charge of the whole place. What did it matter that she had a previous acquaintanceship with one of the attendees?

And that attendee was certainly taking his time in getting to the lodge. When the Lexus finally pulled up, Charlotte watched the grad student sprint out to meet His Majesty before he was out of the car. Gestures suggested complicated explanations. Then he left her at his car unpacking what looked like workshop materials.

Okay, this time is it, Charlotte coached herself. She would greet O.T. halfway to the main door. A meet-cute right out of a romance unfolded in her mind. *A glance and a few words would lead to recognition, then—*

She walked toward him.

"Welcome to Blackbird!" she said holding out her arms for a queenly embrace.

"Sure, thanks."

He went right by her with just a nod, intent on walking to the lake overlook. His hand wasn't available for even a handshake because of his vape.

"Charlotte?" The hand on her shoulder was Will's. "Can you show the lodge rooms for our guests, ahh, Dr. Galesberg, Dr. Bookman, and Ms. Cynthia?" He read off a list. "Or should I?" He spoke in a steadying tone as if her hesitation was triggered by their literary prominence.

"Of course, I'll do it," she said, her tone sharp as if he'd asked who would change the cat box.

She led the group into the lodge, issuing welcome chit-chat to Cinny and Lydia. O.T. turned away from the lake and lumbered along next to Will who asked about the route through Massachusetts.

———— • ————

7

A Dinner Bell and an Alarm Bell

At five-thirty Charlotte toured the dining room one more time and set a bouquet of daisies and fern fronds on the sideboard. She confirmed that the place settings were distributed nicely at large tables convenient for serving family style. Two bottles of red wine with glasses stood on the sideboard from which people could serve themselves. The week's budget allowed only two bottles per dinner. She was laying out napkins when the grad student flounced in with handwritten place cards she distributed, moving O.T.'s three times.

"Dinner's at six, right?" The young woman consulted her watch. "Okay?"

"When dinner is served, Cynthia, I will ring the bell."

Blackbird's schedule wasn't going to be run by someone's smartwatch alarm. The dinner bell was part of the friendly spirit Will insisted on. Anticipation encouraged guests to socialize on the porch while they waited for the clang of the bell that hung by the kitchen door.

Cinny's departure left Charlotte thinking about the weirdness of O.T.'s still having grad student assistants or whatever else they might be. *Did the paisley couch go with him to his Boston office?* She looked at the pushy young woman in tattoos. *Not O.T.'s type.* But this was silly. She was giving him no credit for changing or maturing. She herself had changed since those days, from optimistic ingenue to—

"Your hair!" Will's shout came from the kitchen. "Go show that to your mother."

Green this time? Charlotte braced herself.

Two young men came through the swing door separating the kitchen and dining room. Then she realized the first one was Alice. Her hair was now a brown flap dripping over her right eye and ear, the hair on the other side hardly more than stubble exposing the delicate lines of her skull. The second person, presumably Roy, had curls enough for a drummer in a rock band.

"Mom, don't freak! You're holding dishes." Alice took the plates from her.

"Is that the style now?" Charlotte knew she sounded cold.

"It's easier for summer, don't you think?"

What Charlotte thought was that from the shorn side, O.T.'s profile clearly emerged. "You're going to serve guests like that?"

"Mom, hair grows back. But not before dinner." Alice elbowed Roy.

"Okay. It's very, well, easy as you say." Charlotte pivoted Alice to see the whole effect. "You know, a hat would look very cute, like the Yankees cap."

"Get over it, Mom." Alice's eyebrows rose dangerously. Charlotte retreated.

After all, if Alice didn't serve, she would have to. *And the loss was only hair, formerly lush with gold highlights in the waves that . . .* She repressed more adjectives.

"Well, honey, why don't you show Roy where, uh, they can eat on the porch while you do dinner."

Alice blew her a kiss and put on her lodge apron.

☛

Dinner was a success. As Charlotte refilled serving dishes, she could hear polite discourse and O.T.'s voice rising often with a writerly quip. She kept out of sight. Will asked if she was feeling all right after the hair ordeal. He looked drained and bumped into her twice in the path between the stove and serving counter.

At the edge of the swing door, Charlotte could see into the dining room. When Will brought out the dessert, Lydia led everyone in applause over the compotes of peach-topped pastry. Alice stood ready with vanilla ice cream. Several women asked Will about the herbs he chose for the main course, commenting on the tenderness of the old-fashioned Swiss steak and on the lovely bouquet on the sideboard. Ruth and Bea admired Alice's hair. "So practical for summer," they said. Will hugged Alice and allowed that for the floral nicety, they must thank his dear wife.

Cringing at the domestic helpmeet label, Charlotte knew he meant that as a signal for her to come out, but she stayed put. Finally, he offered his usual historic tidbit.

"Peach cobbler was my mother's Sunday tradition at Blackbird Lodge." He closed with how this dessert was a "known favorite at the Camp Sagamore in the late 1880s." The clanking of serving spoons followed as diners reached in family style to serve themselves.

———— • ————

8

A Post–Peach Cobbler Surprise

Cinny herded the group into the living room after dinner, satisfied with the how the meal went. Her seating arrangements had distributed the talkative seniors and kept the annoying ones next to each other. O.T.'s dinner companions treated him with great respect. They gushed with questions.

"How did he get ideas for his books?"

"What was he working on now?"

"Did he think people were born with talent?"

With each answer he aimed the full effect of his blue gaze. He and the ex addressed each other pleasantly twice from their tables. *Maybe things would turn out all right on that front,* Cinny thought. She needed all the right forces and timing to come together before the New York editor Zenobia Daly arrived later in the week.

Cinny set a rocker in front of the window for the evening's short reading. Of course, O.T. would like to vape and have a drink in his hand, but no smoking of any kind was allowed in the lodge, and no brandy had appeared on the sideboard. He'd have to do without until she could arrange for a break where they could sneak off to the porch for a hit.

She sketched a scenario. *The wind might make it hard to light a joint, which would necessitate their hands brushing, which could be followed by a knowing look after a few inhales, inducing a promise to get together after the writers were tucked in. . . .*

Maybe.

After-dinner malaise was setting in on the writers as they slumped into the overstuffed wicker couch and chairs. She handed O.T. his famous book with a marker for the passage she had chosen. *What are the chances he had read my notes that reminded him to thrill them with the lively pages? Slim.*

Cinny watched Will, attractive in a rugged, woodsy sort of way. His bitchy wife didn't seem like the natural match for the manly innkeeper, something else to hash over with Mina later.

From his rocker, with the sunset a perfect tableau, O.T. read a chapter, languidly letting each phrase work magic. Ignoring her page suggestions, he chose a passage alluding to the fragility of life. He needed to be reminded to keep things upbeat for this group since some were looking death in the eye, maybe Bea, who walked with a cane.

During the reading Cinny studied Westley, the one male attendee, noting his cringeworthy behavior. Though he listened to O.T. and jotted on a small pad, his attention on Lydia was very acute. Lydia, however, didn't seem to notice him. She was animated during the reading, joining the writers in a chuckle or sigh. *Figures.* She had probably heard this chapter a hundred times. Cinny saw a shadow of disgust cross her face after one section. No doubt the passage stirred up an old marital wound. When the reading was over, she decided she would allow about fifteen minutes for comments and then explain tomorrow's warm-up writing exercise before excusing herself and O.T.

☙

Earlier, while Cinny had been arranging chairs before the reading, Charlotte was taking her time prepping the hot drinks in the dining room, and Lydia came in.

"Would you like to join us for O.T.'s reading?" Lydia had changed into an Indian print tunic and pulled her hair back into a topknot that let loose some tendrils.

The woman's joie de vivre added to the glow cast by her book prize and the effect was somewhat intimidating. Charlotte covered her unease with a pleasantry: "The fresh coffee and tea will be ready in a minute."

"Perfect! O.T. will need a jolt." Lydia laughed. "You'll see he's got something in his hand all day long." She spoke as if supervising him was their shared responsibility.

"Oh?" In fact, this was how Charlotte recalled him, a cup, flask, shot glass, or can nearby. Of course, back then stimulants were part of the whole writer thing, not a risk behavior.

"But maybe he's changed," Lydia went on. "He's my ex, you know. Perhaps his new companion has straightened him out." She added with a raised eyebrow, "What do you think are the chances?"

Charlotte yanked her hand away from the spigot of the old-fashioned urn as scalding liquid splashed her wrist. "Dr. Bookman was your husband?"

"Years ago. About the time he wrote that damn book that made his reputation."

"When he was at Ann—" The room faded out from the edges and Charlotte tried to focus on the coffee mugs.

"What a coincidence we should both show up here! He claims that grad student set up the whole thing without knowing." Lydia rolled her eyes.

"The program agency didn't give me any names much ahead of time." Charlotte saw culpability in this potential for fireworks. Would they argue and leave early? Would the lodge have to issue refunds?

"Don't worry, it's not your fault. Besides, this matchup could make it a jolly week." She repositioned a hair comb. "Come on in to listen! You won't be sorry. He's still handsome as sin, if nothing else."

Charlotte felt Lydia's arm sweep her toward the living room as her mind churned on this astonishing news.

In the voice that she knew so well, O.T. read, to the thrill of the group. Heads tipped sideways, half smiles appeared, backs straightened. Charlotte understood. This was what the people had come for after all, had paid the Adamsleys for—to be in the presence of someone wonderful, someone who would help them work magic on their writing in the days to come. Too old to sit at his feet, the writers leaned forward on the lumpy cushions taking in every word. Their hope was contagious, and Charlotte felt the manuscript under her bed send her a callout too.

🍃

At the conclusion of the reading, Cinny broke into the admiring sighs by announcing an assignment that was due in the morning. "Write about a 'first' in your life," she said. "About five hundred words."

A flurry of questions erupted.

"By noon?"

"How long?"

"Were Dr. Lydia or Dr. Bookman going to grade these?"

Cinny smirked. They were just like her freshman comp class.

🍃

As the writers' anxiety frothed, O.T. wondered whether eight o'clock was too early to excuse himself. After all he should set a self-disciplined routine right from the start. First a call to Luella, who would describe Maddie's day. More details than he needed, but he was super daddy this time, and she was his little sugar plum. Then he would turn to his manuscript for a couple of hours. The drive across Massachusetts had given him time for reflection, though encountering Lydia had dampened his enthusiasm for work. Maybe a walk down to the dock for a vape might help him revive.

He gave a thumbs-up to the group and went out on the porch and down the steps. He heard Cinny patter along behind him, an annoying slip-slap of her sandals. She would break her neck—this wasn't Daytona Beach.

"How's it going?" she said.

Did she mean the workshop, or was she poking into whether he was mad about Lydia? "The group seems very enthusiastic." *No need to discuss the ex with her.*

"Would you like to see the outline for tomorrow?"

His time for writing would be nibbled away if he weren't careful. "I'm sure you have things under control." The hint at closure encouraged her instead.

"We'll quickly skim the first assignment right off after breakfast. Then I'll give them another prompt to take up the next two hours. After lunch you, me, and uh, Dr. Lydia will lead crit sessions." She was looking at him. "Any other ideas?"

"Just tell them to write what they know, show not tell. That sort of thing."

He lit his pipe and pointedly contemplated the sun touching the tops of spruces across the lake, hoping she would understand this was the signal that he was excusing her. The sky was gray blue with a few strands of pink.

She inhaled audibly. *A bad sign.* The extra oxygen might give her courage to bring up her manuscript. He had already used up every other excuse for not reviewing her manuscript. His class load, his lack of background on the genre (young adult dystopia, she said), even a headache on one occasion. It was one thing to read this stuff when she had been in his seminar, but that responsibility was over. She was a clever writer, but she was also needy in a dangerous sort of way. He headed off her probable next sentence.

"I hope to get a lot done this week on my book." He made fists as if working out to show his readiness for the challenge. "So, I think I'll turn in." He headed up the steps to the lodge then stopped saying, "Watch those shoes, so you don't fall. Can't have you laid up."

Dealing with these charming workshoppers on his own was not in the cards.

———— • ————

9

First Assignment Anxiety

THE WRITERS, WHO HAD EXPECTED a free Sunday evening, toiled over their first assignment. "Write about a 'first,'" Cinny had said. "Even just a few paragraphs will be all right—let yourself go."

In Bluebird, Ruth paced around. "I was planning on cards tonight."

Cards were a good way to get to know your companions because games brought out their essence. People played recklessly, deviously, hesitantly, confidently, and so forth, and won or lost with grace or anger. Since no cards had been played yet, she'd had to judge by other means. The way people ate also spoke loudly to Ruth, particularly in this setting, since the dining room was intimate with family-sized tables.

Ruth reviewed her findings of her tablemates. Sarah, a striking woman, though clearly depressed, was used to serving others and held the dishes for tablemates. She was considerate about making sure the dressing followed the salad. Westley was another story. It was like playing "Mother, may I?" to get the butter that was near him, then the sauce, then the salt, and finally the pepper. When the rolls arrived, he took two, ignoring that the table was one short. Ruth had him sized up by dessert as a storyteller and not the literary kind.

Millicent, dressed up in a crisp floral shirt and matched sweater for Sunday dinner, talked with such animation that the dishes were like a six-car pileup on the side of her plate. Unlike Westley, she would apologize and send them along, then begin a new story about other workshops, friends, and so forth.

"You know, that Westley is hiding something," Bea said.

Ruth knew Bea's teacher's instinct for sniffing out miscreants and ill-begotten plans had not faded in retirement. "What do you think it is?"

"Not sure, but when a boy hasn't done his homework, he's always quick to tell you he has."

"So, you don't think he's published all the stories he mentioned?" Ruth settled on the couch.

"Something like that."

"Let's keep him on our radar." This was a joke between them, retirees from teaching and social work, a perfect combination in terms of intuition.

They got out notebooks for the assignment. Bea decided to write about her first published writing, a recipe in the weekly paper. Ruth chose her first rejection note.

"We might smoke out something from Westley with these stories. He won't be able to resist telling about his own triumphs."

"Do you suppose Dr. O.T. and Dr. Lydia will write too?" Bea said flipping to a new page. "You can bet it won't be about their first kiss."

"What about that girl, Cinny?" Ruth said. "First kiss with the prof?"

"On her wish list!"

"O.T. is sort of a hottie," said Bea.

"Oh, go on! You find every man under sixty-five a hottie."

"Well, you can bet O.T. still drives at night." They laughed while settling down with their notebooks.

In the Loon cabin, Sarah made some instant coffee. Her daughters had already called twice and, Sarah hoped, been assured that their mother was trying to get in the spirit. Sarah described the dinner served family style in the dining room. There was Swiss steak, rice, and peas or broccoli. For dessert there was peach cobbler. The food was all very good. . . . Yes, the cabin was nice. . . . Yes, she thought her roommate was nice too. . . . Yes, she had brought the right clothes. . . . With each daughter's mind at rest, Sarah thought about the remainder of the evening.

Though she was exhausted, she owed it to everyone to write the first assignment, but she wasn't sure whether to do so in her notebook or on the new laptop. She had never written anything personal on a computer. She opened the laptop and followed the directions one daughter had written for finding Word. Stan would have done this for her because he was in charge of all technology like the TV, the old computer, and the printer. But of course, he wasn't here. *That is why I'm here.* The laptop gave a promising chime and she found Word. *Without Stan.*

"Write about a 'first.'" The grad student, Cinny, who seemed awfully young to be in charge, had said they could write in "any genre." The definition of genre was something else she wished she could ask Stan, who would have googled for her. She found the virtual assistant off-putting and instead considered texting the daughter who would know this sort of thing. Taking herself "in hand," as her mother would have said, she decided to step outside and see if another writer was nearby who might also be puzzling over genre.

Even better, just up the walkway was a person who looked college age. The young woman turned out to be Alice, the innkeepers' daughter, so Sarah asked her about the term used by the professors.

"I'm not sure what 'genre' means. Do you have any idea?"

"Like, how did they use it?

"Our assignment is to write about a 'first' in five hundred words. Dr. O.T. said to write in any genre we want."

"He means you can write a story, or just a conversation, or a poem. Anything you want." Alice sat on a nearby bench and seemed very willing to talk.

"But the content has to be about a first, a first time, I guess."

What a wonderful age Alice was, at eighteen or nineteen, about to have many first times—a first real boyfriend, first job, first paycheck. So many firsts for her mother too. The first time you realize you aren't the center of your daughter's world anymore, the first time you realize you will not miss certain things about her, the first time she comes back to you, the first time you realize you will leave her behind sometime.

"Getting started is always easier when they give you a specific assignment, you know, write on this topic," the girl said.

"I suppose you're right. Freedom's always hard." Sarah thought about the freedom stretching around her at her house. "So, what would you suggest I write about?"

"Well, it's your first time here. First time eating my dad's peach cobbler. You could describe the appearance, taste, and so forth. You could write a conversation with someone, a daughter or friend." She used sets of air quotes to indicate a conversation.

"That sounds complicated."

"How about telling about buying something unusual. Like, my mom bought herself a scarf at the museum last week. She never spends like that. What have you bought that you never did before? A new sofa? A new car?"

Nothing so expensive had she needed to replace but letting Alice down after so many suggestions would be impolite. "I always wanted a black suit. Other women look so smart in them, you know."

"Why didn't you just get one, then?"

"My husband's father was a rabbi and he always said, 'Sarah, a black suit is for old women.'" Sarah could see him plain as day.

"But that's wrong. Everyone wears black. Anyway, why should you care what he thought about your clothes? I don't get it." She ran her hand over her short hair.

"He was a fine man. I respected his wishes for my husband's sake."

"You never got one, ever?"

"I was shopping with my daughters in New York, and I tried on a black suit."

"Didn't you just love it?" Alice leaned in close, ready for a value adjustment.

"I thought the jacket and skirt looked very good in the shop. Made me look slimmer too. But when I put it on at home, I thought it just felt wrong, so I took that suit back."

"But then what?"

"Six months later Stan, my husband, died of a heart attack." Sarah was about to add that he'd never been sick a day.

"You got a black suit. Your first black suit." Alice nodded.

"Yes."

"I'm sorry about your loss. That's a good story though."

Sarah felt the sentiments were genuine. Stan's father was long gone, but how right he had been. Now she felt like an old woman, a widow at sixty-nine. They were supposed to have their golden years together. Instead, she had a terrific-looking black suit.

"Thank you for your help. Tell you what, check in with me tomorrow. I'll let you know how my 'first' turns out."

The girl ran off to join a lanky-looking boy with straggly hair who was loping toward the dock. He was wearing a black suit coat with shorts that hung to his knees. Sarah watched them while she twiddled with the keyboard. The boy took off his jacket and gave it to Alice. He didn't look like a first boyfriend to Sarah. She stared around the room looking for firsts. First cup of coffee in the morning, first day of first grade, first kiss, first baby—a possibility. She looked at Alice again and began to type. "My Black Suit."

☙

Freed of Cinny, O.T. went upstairs. He paused at Lydia's door, then knocked saying his name.

"Sure, come on in."

"I'm glad you're here on this thing, Lydia." She was arranging papers from her laptop case on a little table by the window. "You brought something to work on?"

"I'm making notes for the last few chapters of a book."

"What kind of book?" A yellow pad was the last item, which she aligned with fussy care on the table.

"I'd rather not discuss it."

"Why? You think I might steal ideas?" he said it lightly but saw it hit her wrong.

"Don't be sophomoric."

This would be a bad way to end the conversation. Besides he was curious about this project. "A biography?"

"Not really. It's more like a memoir." Her vagueness could either be sweet or annoy the hell out of him.

"How can it be like a memoir? It either is one or isn't." But this wasn't exactly true. The newer forms crossed traditional definitions. So, her project could be like a memoir.

"I'll tell you about it later this week, okay?" She was unpacking some clothes, some of which were lacy, he noted.

"Sure, I didn't mean to bully." He'd like to sit down but had received no invitation. He glanced at the bed.

"How about you?" She took the rocker by the window and pointed to the small chair nearby. "Have you got something going?"

"Just a couple of chapters to finish. What with teaching and the baby, I haven't been writing much."

"I understand. Family life takes it out of you. Sometimes the muse just vanishes."

O.T. nodded, but he pictured Luella, who at this very moment had surely opened her laptop, studied notes outlined in a steno pad, and typed out a new chapter from start to finish. He wished he and Lydia were sitting on the porch where he might have sat nearer her on a lounge or stood behind her looking at the darkened lake. A bedroom gave few alternatives other than the obvious. He stood again.

"Have a good night, Lydia."

"You too. It'll be fun to work together this week."

Rising from the rocker, Lydia gave him a quick kiss on the cheek. He knew her well despite the time elapsed since they shared a home, and he sensed some disappointment on her part that he didn't press her for more.

When he got to his room, he took one look at his laptop during a lengthy call to Luella and went to bed.

☙

Millicent decided to write her first assignment in the library where Westley had also settled at a table. He wrote rapidly on a yellow pad.

"Well, what do you think of the first assignment?" she said. A "first" had left her stymied, other than the obvious like "first date" or "first time," and she certainly wasn't going to write about that disappointing event. Perhaps his ideas would help her out.

"Kind of trite." He sighed, adding, "I thought this retreat might be a little more imaginative. I came for a change of scene."

"My thoughts too, still I haven't an idea yet. What do you suggest?" The man was attractive in a pompous sort of way. He wore a silk scarf carelessly knotted with an oxford shirt.

"I couldn't begin to suggest for someone else." He began to close up his pad.

"Oh, come on. Help a girl out." This had worked in college for her chem lab reports. He stayed seated, thawing like most men when asked for advice.

"How about the first time you visited a certain place? You could describe your first impressions—first impressions of the South of France, that sort of thing."

She bet he meant this as a slight, implying her idea of travel was visiting Dollywood. In fact, she had done Paris, but not the South of France. "Good idea. I'll write about my visit to La Tour Eiffel." She beamed her French pronunciation at him.

"I'm sure your piece will be heartfelt." His smile was smirky. "Now, if you'll excuse me." He bowed slightly.

She wondered if that was a swipe, but he was going to get away. "Wait. You didn't tell me what you're writing about!"

Millicent was leaning toward him as if in confidence, yet he almost left without taking the bait, then turned. "I'm doing a write-up of my impressions of the lodge. Its history is most peculiar."

"How fascinating! Do tell."

"Perhaps later in the week. We'll see."

Within a few minutes Millicent put pen to paper and surprised herself by writing with gusto in the quiet room. Even though the breeze brought in fresh lake air and the chirruping of crickets, she felt Paris, the gray skies and honking traffic. She described how her tour group had shouldered through the ticket line at the Eiffel Tower, following the umbrella of their guide to the elevator. She felt again her discomfort at being shoved into groups who surely weren't Parisian but South Asian, Middle Eastern, and African—a cacophony of languages and cultures, where she realized being so obviously an American was not an advantage.

At one point, Millicent looked up to find all the lights dimmed in the rest of the downstairs. She could not believe it was midnight, and she was only half into her first assignment. There was so much to say.

✎

With the lodge settled down, Charlotte was about to check Alice's room to see if she was there. She had a few words to say about her shorn head, then remembered Roy with plentiful hair would be in the bottom bunk. This was no time to bring it up.

In her little office, Charlotte sat at her desk processing the Lydia and O.T. relationship, and flaying herself for not googling more about the writers, but what would have been the results? Nothing, other than knowing before Lydia's arrival that this was the woman whom she had discounted as insignificant during her romance with O.T. He had claimed that it was over with his wife. No doubt this disclosure had been just as handy to use with other girls once Charlotte had left. Now it appeared he discounted her so effectively that he didn't recognize her at all.

She got out some wedding snapshots. Just how much had she changed in the years between Ann Arbor and the present? The poses showed her radiant but Will a little shell-shocked, the ceremony coming only weeks after the large funeral the village gave for his parents. Her parents had found her choice of Will odd, but they barely hid their relief at passing to someone else a daughter devoted to endless education. They made no analysis of Alice's early arrival other than complaints about how far their granddaughter was from the Midwest. That Charlotte now had a life other than writing seemed perfect to them.

Charlotte focused on the real issue at hand, considering her options for revelation. Probably Will was waiting up for her in the bedroom. *Maybe this was a good time to explain everything,* she decided. Her resolve hardened until she heard a night bird's descending three-note call.

"There's irony, the whip-poor-will, an omen of ill luck."

She threw herself back into the chair. Resolve dissolved. *No, not yet.* It would upset the rhythm of lodge management to have Will on the lookout. Since she found that the proximity of Alice to O.T. dismaying, surely Will would feel intensely disconcerted if he knew about the relationship.

What about Alice? She rarely asked details about her parents' lives. Springing a clueless biological father on her would be pointless and might distress her, Will, and doubtless O.T. and Lydia. Charlotte closed her eyes. It didn't matter that the knowledge and dread was like carrying a bag of wet sand alone. Will's and Alice's feelings were more important, always. The knowledge was her penance.

When she got to their room, Will was already asleep. She really could have used a little loving from him, reassurance, though given unwittingly.

———— • ————

10

— MONDAY —

Truth Versus Art

THE SENIOR CITIZENS WERE NOT AT ALL what Cinny was expecting. She hadn't been around old people much, other than her grandparents, octogenarians who watched a lot of television. This group argued about the Oscars, checked their social media more than she did, told risqué jokes, and discussed books with vigor. She could tell they wouldn't need the long nap she had planned for the afternoons, time she had pictured herself sunning, writing her book, or boating with O.T.

Gathered in the library Monday after lunch, they shifted around like pigeons, glancing at each other's notebooks or papers, adjusting their sweaters, and giving her the eye when she announced, "We're going to practice a three-step criticism." This was her winning opening exercise with her comp classes.

"Criticism? I thought we were just going to read aloud." A laptop shut with a snap.

Cinny defined criticism again, reminding them that a film critic would elaborate on the strengths and not just the weaknesses of a film. Weaknesses are pointed out to help with change and improvement.

"Isn't that why we are all here?" She looked at each writer, then cut the tension by opening a plastic container of homemade dessert bars. She passed out napkins and offered the container telling the writers, "Don't eat yet."

"Now, what can you say about my creative effort by observing? That's step one." She demonstrated, scrutinizing her treat on its napkin, even checking for aroma.

A flurry of remarks offered that the bars appeared to have nuts or something else crunchy, were chocolate yet smelled of cinnamon, and were darker on the bottom.

Cinny plunged ahead to step two. "And now we will sample." She demonstrated with a large bite and all followed.

"You have sampled my creation, and I'm ready to answer questions." She smiled to suggest her openness.

"Are these brown bits raisins? Maybe next time you should warn us."

The difference between questions and criticism needed review. "Let's hold off any criticisms or suggestions. Just ask questions like 'I'm wondering what the ingredients are.'"

Millicent rephrased. "Oh, sorry. I'm wondering if the chewy bits are raisins."

"Those are chopped dates."

"I'm wondering if there are any kind of tree nuts in here." Lydia had just joined the group.

"Yes, walnuts."

"Do these have a name? Dream bars, perhaps?" Westley held his aloft.

"Chunky cinnamon bars." Cinny improvised since Siri had provided the recipe without an enticing title.

"Chunky? That settles it. I'm not eating more than one," Bea said. Ruth murmured a retort and they both laughed.

After more questions about chocolate type, oil choice, and baking time, they were ready for step three.

"We should always pay attention first to what an artist creates. They have honored us after all." Her flock responded with agreement. "Now, for suggestions you wish to make. But you must first ask if the artist wishes to receive suggestions. Got that?"

"So, this is the criticism part." Millicent began to close her notebook.

In Cinny's experience, this analogy between baking and criticism usually led to worthwhile feedback. Next she would show the magic.

"Sometimes I might not be in the mood to focus on change. But I'm letting you know I am ready for suggestions now." She emphasized "am," which let loose a torrent of suggestions, no surprise, baking not being her forte.

"I prefer a crisp edge."

"The flavor is undefinable."

"Try adding dark chocolate chips."

"Skip the dates, next time."

"Tastes too wholesome."

"A good cook creams in the butter instead of melting to get a lighter center."

"Try spreading on parchment."

And on it went. Cinny thanked each critic, though arguments broke out about nearly all the suggestions. They were all bakers, apparently. She tapped her coffee cup for attention finally.

"When we read or listen to each other, we will be using this format—observation, then questions, then suggestions if the writer wishes. Now, you may have seconds, if you want." Even the critics reached for more before breaking for coffee.

"I didn't come here to be criticized by a bunch of beginners. I can get that at home." Cinny saw Westley close his briefcase.

But coffee gave them the boost to try out the three steps. In response to questions, Millicent said she would add how she felt about being conspicuously American in Paris. Bea's and Ruth's stories about their first publishing efforts brought out calls of "you go girl" and suggestions to insert lines from the publications. Westley "wasn't ready" for suggestions, and Sarah took notes furiously on their questions: "What style was her suit?" "Will she wear it again?"

Cinny congratulated herself on the activity and wished Mina had been there.

☙

During Cinny's session, Charlotte worked at her desk drawing on the workshop deposit to pay outstanding bills. Her mood had shifted from relief at O.T.'s nonrecognition to anger. Had she meant so little that he didn't remember their time together? Or had the years at the lodge aged her too much to be recognizable?

Will ambled in, disturbing a train of thought that included her accusing O.T. of outright abandonment. Her mood was ripe for argument.

"Char, I meant to ask. Anything in the guest books from the Douglasses? About the food or—"

"The lemon bars were a hit with Lucille and Raymond." She didn't mention the tough roast beef because she had suggested to change the cut from ribeye to bottom round.

"Yeah? Anything else?"

"Oh, yes, from Tabby." Disdain crept into her voice. The woman had never been friendly to her. "'Being at Blackbird is always Auld Lang Syne.' That's a quote, and something about comfort food."

He didn't say anything.

"That's a slam on the menu, I think. Cinnamon rolls instead of lobster rolls." His tic of irritation, a slight squint, appeared but she went on with her elucidation. "'Auld' acquaintances. Like the menu, see?"

"Quite possibly." He left the room, not taking up the bait for another argument about the menu.

His attitude made her feel like joining the writers' session scheduled for midafternoon. After all, Lydia had invited her, and so when the time came, she placed a chair on the edge of the group. The topic was figurative language. O.T. looked as if he had just gotten up from a nap, so Lydia began with a definition and read a few recognizable examples. She handed around some dull sentences to rewrite. Everyone worked furiously, reading aloud with mirth and compliments.

Sarah referred to figurative language in O.T.'s book, which brought him to life, naturally, and Ruth also mentioned passages of his that she liked.

Charlotte told herself to exercise restraint but failed. "I'm curious about the next part in that scene Ruth mentioned. If I recall, it goes this way." She quoted the passage by heart to murmurs of approval.

"What made you think of such an unusual analogy for love?" She remembered every pencil stroke of providing this line for his manuscript. *His office cozy with candles and music. The couch—*

"Absolutely perfect, a fearsome phrase," Ruth said before he responded.

"And erotic." Millicent laid a hand on her cheek.

"I'm not sure, really, anymore." O.T. glanced toward Charlotte. "You find it apt?"

"A striking image for passion." She looked directly at him, but his gaze was already elsewhere.

"Well, I appreciate all of your enthusiasm." He sent a boyish smile toward Lydia.

Lydia noticed that Charlotte showed rapt, if somewhat wistful attention. She knew the look meant a writerly yearning. Just as she was about to launch a new group topic, Sarah turned to O.T. asking about how personal experience contributed to good storytelling.

"People will say, 'Sarah, you should put that in a story.' But my retelling turns out to be boring or even slanderous."

"Yes, how can that work out well?" Lydia echoed making it impossible for O.T. to disappear as she could see was his intent.

"You follow where the idea takes you. You can use feelings and impressions from your personal experience without applying them to the same people. In fact, real life recreated on the page is usually rather lifeless." He resettled in his chair.

"Suppose we described in factual narrative this last hour moment for moment. Wouldn't that make dull reading? 'The writers talked about figurative language.' However, if we write from the angle of one person's perspective, the scene would be richer, and we would get to know individuals."

His voice warmed as he began demonstrating points of view with various group members. *Lucky for you, they're wearing name tags*, Lydia thought as he worked his way around the group.

"Bea yawned. The guy had said enough and was eating into her bridge time. Or, Cynthia got out her phone hoping her boss wouldn't notice. Or how's this one: Lydia thought he was overplaying as lead author and wished he would just shut up." He grinned at her. "And the inn mistress, Charlotte, is it?" She nodded slightly. "She's wishing something . . ." He stopped to laugh along with the group.

He's in his element now, Lydia observed. She knew his pleasure was legitimate. He was always a popular and attentive teacher.

"Isn't this changing the truth of what had actually happened?" Millicent said as others agreed these versions were much more interesting.

He snapped his fingers, pointing at Millicent. "Good question! Tomorrow we must have Lydia tell us how she handles experience in memoir where one is assumed to be telling the truth."

Bea and Ruth gave a fist pump of approval. Lydia held his eye and said, "We'll have to define truth first."

———— · ————

11

— TUESDAY —

Something to Chew over before the Pork Chops

Cinny had expected the old folks to have so much trouble with the first assignment that they wouldn't be ready for another one, but unlike the students in her 101 class, they threw themselves into the revisions so well that they were ready to move on.

So, she must invent an assignment on the fly, a creative challenge for the afternoon. After a lunch of vegetable soup and homemade bread, Cinny hunted for interesting items to stimulate their imaginations.

She gathered a few things from under the seat of her car—an old key, a mascara brush, and a birthday party invitation. No doubt O.T.'s or Lydia's car might be a treasure trove but appearing unprepared was not her style. This meant turning to Charlotte for help.

Cinny found the innkeeper mopping the dining room. "Sorry to bother you." She looked irked so maybe a sister-to-sister appeal would work. "I'm in a bit of trouble here?" The mop stopped. "I need some things for a grab bag of writing prompts. Could you possibly—"

"How about the lost-and-found box?" Charlotte dropped the mop entirely and opened a massive cabinet. They pawed under piled sweaters to find balls, an aluminum lunch bucket, and personal items like a razor.

"Maybe not too inspirational," Charlotte said, now much warmer. "Here, empty this." She pulled out a drawer in the hall table rich with forgotten keepsakes, tourist guides and clippings, and writing paraphernalia.

"Perfect! They won't be able to resist this stuff." Cinny added the things to her box and headed to her writers, noticing that Charlotte lingered before retrieving her mop and going to the porch.

"I've got a box here full of objects." Cinny rattled it above her head. "When I come to you, pick three things out. Just grab."

"Do we get to look, or just feel around?" Bea asked. She was the only one that fit Cinny's idea of an old person, and that was only because she walked with a cane.

"You can look for one second."

"What are we going to do with these things?" Millicent looked apprehensive. Others moved closer to try for a peek in the box as they rummaged and kidded before selecting.

"Feels like you cleaned out my desk."

"Are there any blank checks in there?"

The writers whooped as they got objects. Bea and Ruth, who Cinny had noted were inseparable, reached in at the same time.

"Get your hand away from that, girly!" Ruth said and found she had a recipe for making a Manhattan, a barrette, and a queen of clubs.

Bea opened her fist to show a crumpled newspaper clipping, a red pen, and a lead sinker.

"Bet she's going to make us write about these, gang!" Ruth said.

"You took all the good stuff." Millicent stirred up the contents before making her selection.

Westley's enthusiasm suggested he was doing everyone a favor by playing along.

Sarah was last and added drama by covering her eyes.

They groaned as Cinny explained the creative task. They needed to write a longer piece including two objects, one of which must have thematic significance in the story or essay.

Cinny saw Westley try to share a look with her, but she turned away. The guy was a creep and a know-it-all too. Did Lydia notice that he had worked his way to sitting next to her again? Surely, he didn't think Lydia would be interested in him socially. Yesterday after Lydia mentioned point of view, Westley went on and on about POV, showing off with the acronym. Even O.T. held the guy off by humoring him with compliments on a self-serving piece he read.

Bea and Ruth pooled their objects and snatched up the newspaper clipping. Bea pulled a large magnifying glass from her bag, and heads touching, the women bent over the clipping.

Cinny hoped the story wasn't something rude—she should have read it—but she shook off her worry until Bea said, "Ooh, a murder right here!"

Ruth read aloud, "Old Forge, New York. The body found two miles into a marsh off Three Pond Road has been identified as Phillip Cathcart, a guest reported missing from Blackbird Lodge."

"Disappeared last year! Found this year!" Bea interrupted, then elbowed Ruth to continue.

"A sheriff's deputy was led to the remains by a fisherman after his line snagged clothing yesterday. Police speculate Cathcart may have gone to the remote pond without sufficient knowledge of the area and become entrapped by the boggy bottom and weeds. Fishing gear was tangled around the body. Foul play has not been ruled out."

A variety of comments arose around the room about the dates in question.

"Oh, God! Ah, gosh." Cinny lunged for the clipping. "Let's just exchange this for something else."

Ruth's fingers pressed firmly on the newsprint. "No. We'll keep it."

"Yes," Bea offered. "Very amusing."

Pinned down by the questions of other writers, Cinny watched Bea and Ruth move quickly, unusually so for them, out of view into the hallway.

✒

"I think we've got ourselves a plot here, Ruth."

"Right on!"

"Nobody says that anymore." Bea steered them toward the library. "I wonder if the lodge has tried to keep this hushed up."

"You bet. 'Guest turns up missing. Locals mystified.'" Ruth shook her head adding, "Bad for business."

"Let's go find Will to see if he knows whether the cause of death was determined."

Bea's mind was racing ahead. She could already see their crime novel in bookstores, the cover a dark sky hanging over a marsh, a submerged arm with a finger pointing skyward. If they could write fast enough, they could get ahead of the bad report from her last medical scan. Though the upcoming surgery was expected to be effective, she had decided to leave her condition behind at home. For now, her mantra was "see no evil, hear no evil, speak no evil." She hadn't even told Ruth.

In the kitchen Will was preparing alone for Tuesday pork chop night. His focus was on the menu sides: potatoes au gratin, green beans, baby lettuce salad, to be followed by make-your-own ice cream sundaes midevening. An argument with Charlotte about updating the menu replayed in his mind as he prepared the greens. She wanted him to grill outside on a big rig they couldn't afford.

"People don't eat like the postwar baby boom anymore, Will. Stuffed pork chops in the summer?"

He reminded her again that Blackbird Lodge was about tradition. Little flags and sparklers on July Fourth. Evening games on the porch. *And a bit of sag in the mattress.* He laughed out loud. Family style was what people expected at an old-fashioned mountain resort. Even the county health inspector got the point and bent the rules to allow serving plates to be passed around.

Will moved on to the green beans, emphasizing his main point to an invisible audience with his serrated knife. *Blackbird might be the only time some families ate all together other than Thanksgiving.*

"And for that I bet they go to a restaurant!" he said giving the beans a mighty chop. Tuesdays would be stuffed pork chops just like his father served. Moving the ice cream to the dock from the porch was concession enough for him. Of course, in the old days, part of the fun for guests was churning the ice cream. Today he pressed a button on the appliance with a flourish.

The sound of the swing door opening brought his attention to the present. Not Charlotte, but two guests came in exclaiming over the blueberry pancakes from breakfast.

"Light as a feather . . ."

"Positively yummy . . ."

"A family recipe?"

They oozed enthusiasm for one of his old favorites.

He had hardly answered before they moved to examine the stove, a secondhand, six-burner model, and then admired his knife block. "Now, what kind of wood is that?"

He supposed walnut.

The thinner one, Ruth according to her name tag said, "Can you tell us any more about the death of Phillip Cathcart?"

So, this is their business here. "Can't say as there's much to tell."

They waited for more.

"The man was scheduled here for two full weeks and then he disappeared in the second week. We assumed he had driven somewhere else."

"You mean on a side trip?"

"Yep, that's what we thought. Car was gone. Belongings were here."

Because the women stayed put as he tossed the beans in oil and garlic, he explained how after a week passed and the man hadn't come back, they reported his absence to the police who put out a search, but nothing turned up for months. His family had no word either. Then the body was found this spring.

"This must have caused quite a stir for you here," Bea said. "He stayed in the Cardinal cabin?"

"Bluebird." Regretting this revelation, Will went on, "He liked the view of the lake. Stayed here three years in a row. He was writing a book, my wife said."

"Really!" Ruth clapped her hands to her face. "I wonder what kind?"

"Don't know. There was no manuscript in the cabin that I remember."

"How fascinating." Bea moved very close to him as he worked over the beans. "What do you think really happened to him?" Her eyes, open wide enough to smooth out some of the wrinkles, forced him to go on.

"Fishing accident, drowned alone. Happens every summer in the remote ponds, especially to newcomers." He washed his hands, hoping the women would take this hint as their dismissal.

He didn't need to relive the details. The whole thing had upset the rhythm of the lodge and caused cancellations. Charlotte insisted Alice sleep in their room for weeks in case a madman was on the loose. The sheriff deputies poked around, but even if Cathcart were found with his head bashed in, it might be declared "accidental death." Will had his own theories related to guys who didn't take kindly to strangers in their private fishing spot.

"I've got to get to work now. You'll have to excuse me, ladies." He had to peel the potatoes. Charlotte could complain all she wanted, but guests did love his potatoes au gratin.

☛

Ruth yawned conspicuously when they ran into some other writers, announcing naptime for them. They stayed quiet until they reached their cabin where they turned on the rotating fan and moved chairs in front of the window.

Bea lowered herself into the rocker and pulled her blouse open to the fan. "What would Miss Marple do, Ruthie?"

"That's a little like WWJD."

"People used to wear those letters on a bracelet as a reminder for good behavior. 'What would Jesus do?'" Bea flapped the edges of her blouse to collect cool air.

"A good question for us would be WWMMD?" Ruth smirked saying, "Get it?"

"What would Miss Marple do?"

"Right you are!" Ruth gently clapped Bea on the back. "The savior for old detectives like us. I think Chef Will knows more than he let on."

Bea moved even closer to the fan. "He's afraid of scandal at his precious inn, so he helped the whole thing just go away. He told the cops, 'No, we didn't see anything unusual. No, I have no idea, can't think of any reason.'" Bea pantomimed cluelessness.

"What about wife Charlotte? A mismatch for Will, seems to me."

"She wanders around here with her mind elsewhere, haven't you noticed?" Bea flapped her shirt again. "Hand me that pamphlet, or whatever, on the desk. I need a fan."

"This? You want to fan yourself with the guest book from Bluebird, Miss Bea Marple?"

"Well, well, well. Something always pops up. Let's see what's written here from Mr. Cathcart." Bea began to thumb the pages.

"You think entries from last summer are still in here?"

"Bet you dollars to doughnuts."

Ruth listened while Bea read aloud names and dates until, there they were, Phillip Cathcart's entries.

"He's quite loquacious in a guest book," Ruth said.

"He's a writer. This is a form of publication after all."

Bea angled the pages for better light and began to read.

"Tuesday. Rain today, so I stayed in my cabin snug as a bug in a rug and worked on the manuscript. The Tuesday stuffed pork chops were perfect to ward off chill.

"Wednesday. I wrote in the library until the sky cleared and took a long drive. Went north to look at Mount Marcy for inspiration and revised ten pages at a café.

"Thursday. I tried some fishing this morning. The little bay brought me some good ideas for my murder scene but no fish!

"Friday. I spent the morning at the museum and the afternoon writing at the café again. Thanks for the box lunch, Charlotte!

"Saturday. A good day alone with my pen so I went out in the evening. I met some local color at a saloon. He had a story to tell about his relations, quite a blatherskite. Gave me plot ideas for my book and a fishing spot to try. Good company around here!"

"We should have such luck." Ruth interrupted her friend's dramatic reading, but let her go on.

"Monday and Tuesday. More rain. Etcetera. He liked the dinner," Bea summarized, adding, "He hit a bad week for weather. Good thing he's got revising to keep him occupied. Okay, here's something."

"Read on, Macduff." Ruth sat forward.

"Wednesday. Cloudy. I think I'll try out the fishing spot I heard about the other night. Could be just a fish story! Don't want to end up lost or in a pine overcoat."

"A pine overcoat?" Bea set down the book.

"A coffin. How's that for a premonition?"

Their brainstorming session made them miss teatime while they made notes for a book plot that led to the untimely and, they hoped yet-to-be-uncovered, ending of Phillip Cathcart.

☙

During her Tuesday cleaning tasks, Charlotte pondered the cache of writing prompts, how the ordinary could draw out the extraordinary. Perhaps she would hear some results in the evening. For the next hour she could tend to her garden along the driveway where there was enough full sun for a short season of flowers and herbs. A Midwesterner, she had not realized how much work even this small garden would require in the rocky soil. After much composting and mulching, protective leaves in winter, and fertilizer, she had coaxed along annuals, a few favorite perennials, and kitchen herbs and greens. The output was as difficult as the writing and parenting, and with the same results: something that grew to be more exuberant than she expected, making her forget the labor she had put in.

The impulse to plan for next year was automatic. She pulled off dry zinnia heads to collect the seeds, putting each color in a separate bag. Traveling the garden rows made her think of other paths. Suppose she had told O.T. about the pregnancy? He might have taken her on somehow or at least paid child support. *But no abortion, what with his seed involved and his ego.*

Might she and Alice be living with him in Boston now, as wife and daughter? She looked beyond her garden at the rugged ground that had seemed inhospitable. Now she knew the floor under the hardwoods and conifers was rich with curiosities like Indian pipe, dwarf rattlesnake plantain, even orchids, and Alpine flowers in the High Peaks. The mountains folded in the distance like a blue-green, brooding sea. Truth was, the landscape suited the person she had become.

"Mom!" Alice came along the path, a nice surprise. "Mom, here's some news. Patsy's getting married."

"She's not going back to college?"

"She's pregnant. I don't get it. There's a million ways not to get pregnant."

Charlotte nodded wondering how firsthand this knowledge was.

Alice went on, "Babies are cute, but you just look so stuck, if you know what I mean."

Charlotte smiled. How unmindful Alice was that this remark touched on her own history. They walked along a row of green tomatoes that might or might not get a chance to ripen. Alice picked one, tossed it high, and caught it.

"Do you ever think about 'could ofs'?" Alice missed on her second throw.

Charlotte wanted to correct her with "could have been," but said, "As in?"

"Okay, suppose, you didn't marry Dad? It could of," she emphasized for clarity, "been just you and me, or even you and me and mystery DNA donor."

"Mystery!" The implication that Alice's conception was a hookup rankled Charlotte more than the grammatical error. "I know who the man is. Was." Alice didn't catch the slipup in tense.

"Whatever." She ambled down a row of zinnias. "I'm just thinking about how random my life path is."

"Go on."

"We would have lived somewhere else, if you had done, for instance, B instead of A."

"'A' being marrying your dad?"

"Yeah, and if B, we would have lived wherever the sperm donor is now, maybe Los Angeles, Seattle, or, or Rome!" She opened her arms and spun around as if the missed opportunities were just over the horizon.

"See, random! Life could just as easily have turned out very differently and be just as good. Don't take this the wrong way—but maybe even better. You just don't know when you make a choice." Alice flipped up her hands mimicking cluelessness.

Fortunately, Will wasn't around to hear this philosophical riff. He tended to see his life as moving along a predetermined path.

"Or," Alice turned to her, "you might have gotten an abortion, and I wouldn't be here at all."

Charlotte fiddled with her seed bags to cover the bizarre similarity between her daughter's speculations and her own.

"So, where's this going, Alice?"

"Nowhere. I'm just saying our life could have been a different story." Alice poked a flower behind her naked ear. "You're always going on about 'story.'"

Maybe the moment was right for the big question. "Have you thought you would like to meet your biological father?" She hoped she sounded casual. "Sometime?"

"DNA dad!" Alice's eyes flashed in a facial expression very like one of O.T.'s. "Oh, wow! Meeting him could be cool, if it's okay with Dad and you."

"I think it would be."

Alice's face lit up with a realization. "You know where he is?"

"He was someone I knew in grad school." She dodged the truth, but it felt good passing on this tidbit. Alice shouldn't think she chose partners without discrimination.

"But you know where he is, now? Do you text? Or follow him on social media? Or Facebook?" Alice got out her phone.

"Of course not."

"Does he know where we are?" Alice wasn't going to let the story go this time and unearthed the most tender point. "He does know about me, right?"

Charlotte collected the seed bags and weeds they had pulled.

"Mom?"

Her silence answered the question.

Alice held her eyes, then said, "You never told him! He was already married, huh?"

"I'm not sure how to explain."

Where to begin? The paisley couch? The seduction of the art of words and how her novel and his seemed more important than anything?

"I get it, a long story. It's okay, Mom." Alice put weeds on the compost pile with a fling that said explanations could wait, but not too long. Then she jogged off and waved.

Charlotte lingered. Could Alice's sunny disposition forgive her reticence on the subject of her biological father? And would Alice ever acknowledge that her mother had correctly chosen the path north? Indeed, each choice did have consequences, setting in motion a story with characters and theme. But unlike Alice, Charlotte thought choices were not always made at random but were instead inevitable, having been set in motion by other forces. Alice's view, that one was always free to choose, was a function of her youth. Time and experience had shown Charlotte otherwise.

She watched as Alice jogged down the road and got in her car. If she were going back to Albany to visit Roy, she would have said so. Or so Charlotte hoped.

———— · ————

12

An Assignment in NYC

WHILE CHARLOTTE WAS TENDING HER GARDEN, in Manhattan Netta Simpson stood in front of the desk of Zenobia Daly, editor-in-chief of Daly House Publishing. Netta, assistant to an assistant editor, was surprised to be called into the inner office and told she was to drive upstate to a writers' retreat.

"A workshop thing for senior citizens, Netta. I agreed to this for PR six months ago, but I can't take the time. You go. Be nice to the old folks, praise their efforts."

"Actually, I have plans to—"

"You want to advance here, or not?"

Netta nodded and glanced through the brochure that had flown across the desk moments before.

Zenobia went on, "Spend a couple of days. Read their little stories, poems, or whatever. Make a few suggestions and direct them to our latest catalog, of course."

Netta scanned the program description. "This says, 'New York editor will critique selections and may bring back proposals to a major publishing house.' What would you like me to look for?"

"The key word is 'may,' 'may bring back,' Netta."

"Seems kind of disingenuous." Her ruined weekend date with a Yale grad made her reckless.

"That's publishing. You should know that by now," Zenobia snapped.

As usual, the woman's manner left Netta unsettled. "Uh, I guess."

The ideas she had when she took the entry-level position with Daly House were now laughable. She had pictured editors hunched companionably over coffee debating the merits of a manuscript, looking for fresh faces, encouraging ingenues while coddling a stable of temperamental stars. Instead, bloodthirsty competition broke out as editors pushed their favorites, hoping to be credited with earning big bucks for the house. Yelling, dramatic exits, even thrown markers and coffee cups occurred during meetings where Netta huddled in the corner as assistant to an assistant editor and was often sent out for more coffee.

"My remark was a joke, Netta, for God's sake. Get a rental car. Go up to Blackbird Lodge, wherever it is, and make a good impression for Daly House."

Zenobia looked directly at her and pointed with a nail file. "We're counting on you."

Netta bobbed her head and backed toward the door with a thank-you-for-your-confidence-in-me sort of exit line.

In her cubicle she sighed. She had thought loving books and knowing a good story would be enough for success in publishing. What counted, though, was recognizing which story would sell. This was hard to learn, it turned out. She glanced at the pile in the corner, a grocery bag filled from the slush pile at Daly House. Unsolicited manuscripts were given to the junior staff to read, while the agented ones went to the senior editors.

In her spare time in her apartment, the time not spent doing laundry in her tiny sink, Netta read the slush pile. Some of

the manuscripts were wonderful. At first, she brought these
to the editors, but then ceased after their reviews.

"Netta, what were you thinking? This book's a piece
of crap."

"Have you actually read any of our best sellers?"

"What did they teach you in your MFA?"

Daly House was not the kind of place to put out a literature
prize winner, Netta wished so much to point out. Most titles
were what she considered barely above airport reading. Yet she
kept alive her fantasy of finding in the slush pile the perfect
book, something beautiful, well written, entertaining, profound
yet uplifting, something that would speak to the times as well
as sell like wildfire. Someday she would find such a book for
Daly House. Or perhaps she would write one herself that
would go into the slush pile and be discovered by one of the
supercilious editors. *No!* She would send her manuscript to
a different house. *And wouldn't Daly House be sorry.*

——— · ———

13

Another Lodge Tradition

AFTER DINNER LYDIA GATHERED THE WRITERS over wine. She explained the importance of story from ancient times to the present and remarked how fortunate it was to be gathered for a week devoted to writing and storytelling.

"Stories help us make sense of our lives. Stories help us explain and accept the tragic and the wonderful. Stories show how we fit into the flow of time."

Bea suggested that stories preserve history for future generations, and Sarah said they might deliver a moral. Heads nodded.

Lydia added, "And stories are for fun and entertainment, of course. The best stories, the ones we remember like *Romeo and Juliet*, 'Chicken Little,' *Gone with the Wind*, or Jesus's parables have the story arc. Basically, that means a beginning with an inciting event, a middle with rising action, and an end that answers a question raised in the story."

She went on to say that this is what they had paid for, to learn how to make their own stories live within the ancient traditions.

Cinny then took over, introducing the night's event. "We're lucky to indulge in the ancient tradition tonight. Mr. Adamsley has agreed to tell us a story. Like people in all places from all times, let's gather round the fire."

The group resettled into the furniture near the fireplace as Will drew up a chair. Alice came in and sat on the floor by him.

"Storytelling was a tradition in these lodges, from what I've read of local history," he said.

Lydia noticed that O.T. had joined them, coming in from the porch, probably after a surreptitious vape.

"Did your family build this lodge?" Westley's tone suggested polite interest.

"The Adamsleys do go way back in the area, but we acquired Blackbird in the early 1930s from the Whitehead family. They were New York real estate magnates."

"I guess times were hard for the wealthy, too, if they sold this beautiful place," Ruth said.

"Actually, my great-grandfather won the lodge in what you could call a wager."

"No! In cards?" Bea perked up. "I've heard of bets like that."

"Not cards. More like a contest. Mr. Whitehead, the owner, bet his hunting buddies he could tell the best story. What do you think of that?"

"Go on."

"Details, please."

"Do you know the tale?"

Lydia saw the group draw in even closer as Will began to conjure the scene. His skill was a surprise and a welcome bonus to the evening.

"I can see them plain as day—the city friends drinking and gambling every night along with George Adamsley, the property manager, my great-grandfather. The picture out there"—he pointed toward the hall—"shows the Whiteheads in a truck. George is the driver.

"Their last night someone suggested a contest, a contest of stories. They would have a silent vote on the best one, and the winner would get the kitty. Each man wrote down his contribution to the kitty."

"Oh, think of that. Right here in this room," Millicent said.

"Probably the wind came up, it was November hunting season, and I suppose they hauled in more wood. Some of the men were sleeping downstairs because of the cold. Whitehead had the only other stove in his room upstairs overlooking the lake.

"Well, now, as my daddy heard it, one of the men told a story from the Great War. Another told how his people crossed from Ireland in the potato famine. Whitehead told about an African hunting trip."

Alice spoke up. "Dad, don't forget about the *Titanic*. One guy's grandmother had been saved in a lifeboat."

"Glad I have my backup here." Everyone laughed. Lydia could see the girl was completely engaged with her father's telling.

"The estate manager, remember that was George Adamsley, told about the woman in white seen in the upstairs hall at least once a year."

A collective gasp brought the group even closer.

"According to his story, she's looking for her son Ethan who was visiting cousins here in 1895. He died in a measles outbreak and was quickly buried out back—grave's still there. His mother arrived too late, and when she saw the grave, she threw herself in the lake."

"A lady of the lake! Have you seen her?" Sarah said.

"I've heard her footsteps upstairs." Alice's enthusiasm was as contagious as her father's.

"Which room?" Lydia asked thinking of her bed under the sloped roof.

"Can we visit the grave?"

"Is there a marker?"

Will built the suspense by going on with his tale. "The stories got crazier as the men drank more and the wind picked up moaning through the spruce branches. Finally, they voted as the clock struck midnight."

"That clock right there!" Alice pointed to a pendulum wall clock.

"The votes were counted. Two for the war story, two for the *Titanic*, one each for a couple of others, and three for the lady of the lake." The group cheered, but Will held up his hand. He had more to tell.

"Wait, wait! Don't forget about the notes in the kitty. A couple of the friends offered a hundred dollars apiece. The estate manager, Adamsley, promised his wife's apple pie to the winner, and Whitehead, out of cash assets, promised the lodge."

"No!" Lydia heard herself shriek.

"Ah, a gambler's mistake!" Ruth said.

"He had figured his peers wouldn't want to take on the deteriorating property, even in a wager. Not so the estate manager," Will said slowly. "A gentleman never reneges on a wager, and Mr. Whitehead was a gentleman. And that's how Blackbird Lodge came to the Adamsleys."

No story could be better conceived or told, Lydia thought, wishing Will was a group member as well as host. The remarks of the others echoed her opinion.

"Who would think this sort of thing really happened. It's more like a fairy tale."

"Remarkable."

"Will set the bar high for the rest of us storytellers." Sarah got confirmation from everyone except for Westley who appeared to have dozed off.

"And the tale was well ordered, too, don't you think?" Lydia stood to sum up the evening. "Think about how the teller arranged the story as an arc." She gestured the shape.

They began to postulate but she waved them out of the room. "Sleep on it."

———— • ————

14

—WEDNESDAY—

A Free Afternoon and Evening Disclosure

Ruth and Bea saw Millicent on the library rattan couch hunched over a book. "What's that book you're reading?" They spoke nearly in unison.

"Oh, just a fun read. Nothing heavy."

"A mystery? They can be so engrossing," Bea said as they took seats on either side of Millicent.

"Yes, this one is. Very exciting."

"Who's the author? I have favorites in the genre." Ruth tried to read the book jacket.

"Well, I promised not to say, but the author is one of the workshop participants."

"Oh my!" Bea put a finger on her lips. "Who?"

Millicent looked toward the hall. "Westley. He gave it to me on the q.t."

"I should think he'd want to show it off."

"He was afraid of offending people." Ruth and Bea leaned in as Millicent lowered her voice.

"Sex? Violence?" Ruth whispered.

"No, no, not that. He was worried he would be lording it over the rest of us, him being a published author, and all."

"Ahh, the epitome of modesty, he is." Bea nodded. "I'd love to read the book too. On the q.t., of course. Could I borrow it?"

Millicent glanced around again before handing it over. "Maybe you should read in your cabin."

"Yes, what a good idea." Bea stood and tucked it under her shirt, signaling to Ruth to stand too. They left quickly.

With the writers scattered in the lodge, in their cabins, and even on the dock, O.T. supposed he should make a show of writing himself. He brought downstairs a folder of pages and notes for his manuscript's unfinished conclusion. Lydia was in conversation with Sarah in the living room. As usual, she drew the earnest types and they were talking about the cathartic effects of writing. Lydia was encouraging Sarah to keep a journal, of course. One of the hallmarks of their marriage was Lydia bent over her journal. Not even a screaming fight would deter her from penning her extensive entries.

O.T. went to the dining room sideboard where coffee was set out under a dark oil painting of an elk with a Mona Lisa stare. He poured a mug and added cream and a lot of sugar. A plate of chocolate chip cookies called his attention. Generally, he saved his calories for wine, but this was a vacation of sorts away from Luella's appraisal of when love handles might become a tire. He took two because chocolate had animating effects, after all. For now, carbs would have to replace his preferred muses of gin and Mary Jane.

On the porch, he set his pages on the table with the peeling birch bark legs. He riffled through the printed pages until he found his handwritten notes. These comprised the last twenty typed pages with about ten more in cursive. All were filled with cryptic notes and arrows. He hadn't run this manuscript by anyone yet, hadn't even hinted at the contents to his agent. Maybe his silence was what discouraged her from calling anymore, but she had no idea what went into writing a great book any more than, well, Luella.

"Just follow your notes, Oatie. I'll take the baby out so you can write," she said every Saturday afternoon.

Wine, women, and song. There was truth in the old saying. The old days, his blood singing from pills or booze, late-night bull sessions, sex—these were the keys to creative thinking missing in the cloying routine of second-time-around helpmeet and daddy.

Through the screen door he heard Lydia say gently to the widow, "Perhaps writing will help you let him go peacefully."

She should know, though she claimed that he had left her, which was not true. Technically. After a three-day writing binge that included Christmas Eve at an apartment with female grad students, he had gotten up late Christmas morning and returned home to find the house empty, the tree down, and his gift decorated with a note calling him a selfish prick. *I probably was that year.*

He read the last few printed manuscript pages and went on to the handwritten ones. The story took up the later life of the central character from his first book.

Maybe he could risk an e-cigarette out here, but the inn-keeper's wife—now there's an eye-catching woman—might be in the dining room. No smoking applied to the porch too. He stared at the lake while feeling around inside himself, looking for the jolt, the moment when words would pour out.

Maybe a third cookie would help. O.T. carried his coffee mug back inside despite the danger of being accosted for advice. *Where was Cinny anyway?* She should be walking around encouraging the writers and keeping them away from him.

He moved quickly to the dining room. *Yes, the cookies were still there, but not the woman—Charlotte, was it? Too bad.* He dawdled over a brochure on the history of Blackbird Lodge, playhouse of the rich turned TB asylum and now another sort of asylum: a loony bin this week for people who thought their ideas were so important that they needed to be recorded for posterity. *Me included!* He reprimanded himself.

Back on the porch, he was about to set down the cookie and coffee but at the wrong table since it was empty. Had he been sitting at the round table, the one with dreadful legs made of deer antlers? No, the one with birch legs was where he had left his stuff. Now the manuscript and the handwritten pages were gone.

He backtracked inside. Maybe he had taken the pages on his cookie quest. Not so. The rooms were empty of pages and people to ask. He ran upstairs in hopes that he had imagined carrying the pages downstairs. Sometimes he pictured a scene so clearly that it seemed to have happened, especially after an Adderall, not that he had indulged today. The laptop case was empty of paper, the little desk bare. How about his suitcase? He dumped all his clothes on the bed, but no pages appeared. He checked the dresser drawers, around the toilet—anything was possible. He felt his heart speeding up and a pain in his chest. Was he having a heart attack? He felt like vomiting, a sure sign, or so he had read. He flexed his left hand. No sign of numbness.

Of course, the typescript could be reprinted, but the handwritten pages and the notes on the typescript were gone like the will-o'-the-wisp. How could he woo Zenobia's Daly House without the masterful conclusion?

The pages had to be somewhere. Since men were no good at finding things, he concluded, he needed a woman to fix this. A woman would know where to look. But on the way back downstairs it occurred to him that perhaps a woman took the pages. The house was full of them.

&

Lydia felt at loose ends. She knew the worst thing during a workshop was to get involved with one of the participants, breaking the sacred contract of trust between teacher and student, though she had corresponded with several later and even dated one for a while after the workshop was over.

Since this was a senior group, she had not expected to find any man particularly interesting except for O.T. He was turning out to be elusive, evaporating when personal conversations could develop. Perhaps he was devoting himself to writing or to the graduate student. His style would be to have her type up notes from an audio file or sit for hours while he mused or gave tirades, or perhaps—Lydia flushed—astonished with sexual appetite. He could carry out any number of activities that would surely drain the girl's creative muse while he made her responsible for his own.

Lydia flipped through the manuscript she had brought to the retreat. When they were still married, and after, Lydia wondered if without her setting aside her own aspirations, O.T. would have flourished as he did. Maybe she should take credit for his early successes, though in the long run, he had made the greater sacrifice in missing their sons' babyhoods while he wrote or stayed away. Later he was the part-time father who called or sent gifts, swept in for a visit, or took them for vacations they couldn't really appreciate.

Lydia decided she was through speculating about what O.T. might be doing for the afternoon. Why not walk along the main road to the store at the crossroads? The rhythm of her steps might assist her in mulling over the ending of her manuscript. She got her sunglasses and put cash in her pocket. At the end of the driveway, she found a snowmobile path that ran alongside the road toward the store.

Her book's subject was her marriage to O.T. Naturally she had been vague when he asked about it. She had traced their first year in a communal house on campus, their back-packing across Greece, his indiscretions, the mysterious fire that destroyed her dissertation notes, his disappearance with the boys for a week with a visiting female faculty member, and his numerous gifts for reconciliation. Woven throughout her text were meditations on what happens when people with creative impulses couple—the inherent dangers, plus a few felicities. She included historic examples, Zelda and F. Scott Fitzgerald for one, and speculated on modern ones from Hollywood, such as Richard Burton and Elizabeth Taylor or Angelina Jolie and Brad Pitt.

She kicked a pine cone along the trail, thinking about how the book had no ending yet. *Because we have no ending yet?* The pine cone spun off into the brush. Or rather, she didn't know what O.T.'s ending was yet, so she had no final analysis of him in his relationship to her—parasitic or symbiotic—or to his art. Would he be a literary footnote or an American giant?

Tramping along, she asked herself again, who or what was the book about, really? Her willingness as a woman to be victim in the relationship? Her assumption that his talent was greater than hers, thus her sacrifice for the greater good? The crunch of her footsteps generated adrenaline, pressing her thoughts and steps forward faster. She felt energized knowing both the crossroads and the book's conclusion were not far off.

At the end of the lake was a little town made up of a few rental cottages, a post office, and a large convenience store with a gas station. In front were a few picnic tables. As she reached the parking lot, she felt someone close behind her. Perhaps O.T. had followed.

"Can I get you an ice cream?" Westley's affected phrasing put the accent on cream. The guy was probably harmless albeit annoying. It was only ice cream, so this wouldn't be breaking her rule against fraternizing.

"Yes, that would be lovely. How about a scoop of chocolate?" He bowed slightly and headed into the store.

He stood out among the writers. At first it was because he was the only man and a published writer, and he had oozed enthusiasm about her last book in a group session. He always wore a silk scarf loosely at his neck and tight Italian-cut trousers, but by the second day her judgment of him had changed from debonair to creepy.

"Here you go, Dr. Lydia." He handed her a tower of ice cream wedged into a rolled cone.

"Goodness, this will spoil my dinner."

"Well, Dr. Lydia, what do you think of the workshop so far?" He leaned forward as if to catch every nuance.

"I'd be more comfortable if you just call me Lydia." She wasn't going to be drawn into comparing notes. The ice cream began to flood over the wilting waffle cone. She tried to keep her licks from seeming lascivious as she worked to prevent the chocolate from running down her hand.

"I appreciate your comments on my style so much, Lydia." The way he said her name now implied the status of colleagues. She regretted her invitation to use her first name.

Had she really commented on his style? As a teacher she believed in saying something positive, even about the worst prose, something like "a very vivid description." She tried for a neutral remark now.

"I hope you're finding the exercises worthwhile, Westley." She longed to add "weasel," Westley Weasel would be perfect for his fluid, silent stride. His eyes were rather close-set too. She drew back a little on the bench.

"Certainly, they are perfectly tailored for the rest of the group." He dug into his own ice cream, which was in a dish. "Most inspiring has been hearing about Dr. O.T.'s latest project."

"His project? His latest book? Oh, yes." O.T. hadn't said anything about his current writing as far as she knew.

"Sounds like a seminal work. Very exciting," he whispered, brow furrowed.

"Oh? In what way?" It didn't seem possible Westley could know anything, but his occasional wittiness might have put him into O.T.'s confidence. An inability to read people had been a perennial problem for O.T., though on the page he could breathe character into a stone.

"I think the ending is just marvelous. Oh, here let me dab that for you."

Chocolate ice cream had dripped on her knee. Westley dunked a napkin into his cup of water and wiped her leg more gently and longer than a drip required.

Lydia could hardly sit still, but courtesy to a workshop participant demanded she end this pleasantly. Maybe the man had knowledge. *Was O.T.'s book really finished?*

"Did you agree with his conclusion?" she said. This guy wouldn't miss an opportunity to show off his value as a critic to the master.

"Lydia!" He continued after a pregnant pause, "As you surely know, O.T.'s endings are always like a clash of cymbals."

Westley raised an eyebrow as if this were a shared intimacy, but his hopes were as wrong as his descriptions of O.T.'s endings. In his best stories—though not in his relationships—the endings were gentle, much more like the fading light of a perfect day.

Lydia stood, satisfied Westley was a liar. "Don't let me keep you from your writing. I see you have a notebook with you."

"This was my pleasure. Perhaps Thursday we can do it again?" The phrase was particularly ill-chosen.

"Thank you for the ice cream today. The schedules are quite full for the rest of the week." She clambered over the picnic table bench before he had a chance to help her and began a very brisk walk back to Blackbird.

The missing manuscript crisis exhausted O.T. so he napped, then realized he had missed dinner and nearly the sharing of the group's revision efforts. He hurried downstairs. The lodge mistress, who was talking with Lydia, whisked out as he surveyed the room for a seat. She seemed to leave whenever he arrived.

"Oh, my!" He sat down checking his phone for the time and shrugged his shoulders to remind everyone he was an absentminded professor.

"Yes, you naughty man. We gave up on you," came from someone near the fireplace.

"We need you to set us right to get ready for the New York editor," added the woman whose name tag read "Bea."

Cinny chimed in with a humorous reproach to him, then said, "Could you talk a little more about point of view? They have asked about first person."

He got the message. Either read her manuscript later or do some of the work now. With half of his attention he rambled on about how first person, though revealing of one character, limited the reader's knowledge and often the truth of the other characters. The other half he devoted to analyzing the group for a culprit or for a psychic who could find the pages.

Maybe Bea was on the dotty side, forgetful or a collector of things like the lady down his block at home. Her friend Ruth looked dismayed as Bea struggled to find something in her bag as he finished his monologue.

"Your notebook's right beside you, Bea. Don't get your panties in a bunch." She elbowed Bea when others laughed.

"I don't know how I put up with this woman." Bea found her notebook, which had many papers protruding. "I wouldn't have you read this drivel for the world," she said gesturing at O.T. and holding her notebook to her chest. "Come on, Ruth. Let's go. Time's a-wasting."

O.T. watched Bea gather up her purse. *Or laundry bag. Whatever it was looked heavy. Had she carried this around before?*

The weather did him a favor by cutting off more discussion. Low-lying clouds turned navy blue over the lake, shifting the atmosphere from cozy to forbidding. The single male writer followed Bea and Ruth out. Others escaped the gloom over the lake by going to the dining room, which was well lit.

Cinny headed toward him, no doubt a book chapter in hand. He wasn't going to get away this time. She had already given him all afternoon free and he had disappeared until the end of the nightly crit session. She assumed he was going into the dining room, but he turned quickly, bumping into her. Before she could say a word or hand over the folder, he bounded up the stairs after Lydia.

☙

"Look, Lydia, I need to talk to you about something." She saw O.T. was already in her doorway looking nervous.

"Yes?" She had been waiting for this moment for years. *He wants to apologize for the shocking way he behaved as a husband. He wants to say how much he liked my last book.*

"It's kind of embarrassing." This didn't sound like a preview to soul-searching. She felt angry with herself for imagining he had changed.

"So, what is it?"

"I was on the porch this afternoon with manuscript for the last chapters of my book and they disappeared."

"Disappeared? Were you drinking?"

"No, coffee and cookies."

He paced around her room explaining how he had stepped away and someone took them.

"Surely, you don't think I took them." She waited for him to answer, which he didn't.

"You probably set them somewhere else and forgot." How many times had she searched their house while he raged at her, the boys, or their housekeeping when one of his notebooks, his keys, even his toothbrush disappeared?

"I'm not getting that senile. I was on the porch with the printed pages, and now they're gone along with my handwritten pages and notes." He flopped on her bed but not under the circumstances she had pictured.

"What about that grad student of yours? Maybe she thought you left them out for her to handle."

"It's not like that with her."

"Sure." She crossed her arms. "Don't worry, tomorrow we'll keep our eye on the writers. Maybe one picked up the pages by mistake. Or the innkeepers. Maybe they were tidying up. Did you ask them?"

"Why would they clear up papers since my stuff was obviously laid out for work?" He checked his phone. "Too late to bother them now."

"You're thinking manuscript theft?" This would be typical of him.

"I don't know what I'm thinking. I just need the pages back."

He stood and she led him to the door and patted his back. Desperation sex wasn't what she was looking for.

————— • —————

15

— THURSDAY —

Rosemary Chicken, Part I

AFTER THE MISSING PAGES HAD PLAGUED O.T. all night, he was tired Thursday morning. His conversation with his women, First and Second, hadn't helped, even making him sorry he'd mentioned the pages at all, especially in a call to Luella since the loss implied incompetence when unsupervised. Also, Facetime with the baby made him realize how much she could change even in a few days. She crooned "meow, meow" when prompted about what the kitty says. How had she learned that? *Without me, apparently.*

The week away would serve for income but no book deal in the long run if he had no notes for polishing the final chapter. He could see the printer at the lodge couldn't handle a job the size of his manuscript, so he would have to drive to the nearest office supply store to reprint the final sections, even unrevised. That could be twenty miles. As Lydia suggested, he should ask the lodge couple about the missing pages before confronting the writers. He was about to open the swing door to the kitchen when he heard raised voices. Domestic discord was no setting to interrupt—*don't*

I know that well—and so he loped to the library to wait out the spat.

Charlotte had come in the back door to the kitchen where Will was simmering onion and potato soups.

"Are you going to slice the chickens in the kitchen tonight?" She already knew his answer.

"No. On the sideboard like always." The tension of watching the soups and pummeling the rising cheesy bread made him perspire.

"But the chicken ends up kind of messy-looking."

"Messy?" He sounded flummoxed.

"If you slice in the kitchen, I could arrange portions and put accoutrements on the platters."

"What the hell are you talking about?" Will finally looked at her directly.

She held up a magazine spread of poultry arranged fan-shaped around nosegays of fresh herbs. "I want the chicken to look more like this."

He glanced at the photo. "You can gussy up platters in here before I carve on the sideboard."

This was as far as he would budge. Then she berated herself. What difference would fancily served chicken make in showing the significance of her North Country life? O.T. didn't remember her, and that's that. The week was a lot simpler because no revelations of any kind were necessary. She had reminded herself fifty times, but even so her regret magnified all minor frustrations. To prove her point that chicken improved with presentation flair, she would arrange translucent lemon slices and little bouquets of rosemary on the platters before they went to the sideboard. *Whether he likes it or not.* To quell her inclination to say more, she began a strenuous rearrangement of the pantry shelves.

☙

What the hell? Will kept his irritation silent. His quick turn prevented the soup kettle from spilling as the dining room swinging door nearly hit it. Bookman was not far behind.

"Yes? Can I help you?"

He forgot Alice's suggestion that he should reform this phrase to "How may I help you?" She said the new wording implied sincere desire to assist, but he was feeling no such desire. This wasn't a call center. There had been no recent catastrophe at the lodge where guests were in dire need of assistance. The fancy professor seemed ready to make himself at home even in the kitchen.

The guy looked around as if the kitchen appliances were an audience. "Well, yes. Lydia, my partner, uh, other leader, thought maybe you could help me."

Will lifted his head but kept working.

"Some manuscript pages I was working on yesterday afternoon went missing from the front porch."

Maybe the knife lying on the cutting board deterred the professor from leaning on the counter, Will thought.

"Missing?" he hefted the kettle back to the stove after adding seasonings. Charlotte's rearrangement activity quieted after the delivery of this news.

"Yes, I went indoors for a few minutes. The materials were gone when I came back." He snapped his fingers as if demonstrating a magic trick.

"A wind, possibly?" Will said over his shoulder as he nestled the bread in pans.

☙

The fact that this babble was implying theft, or something, would not sit well with Will, Charlotte knew. For her part, she recalled many an afternoon where she had scampered around O.T.'s office looking for a misplaced lesson plan, a pile of essays, or even his check. These pages would turn up folded in his pocket by evening. She could see the men through the gap between the pantry door and the jamb.

"I searched my room, you know, in case of a mix-up on my part." O.T. gestured confusion and went on, "I wondered if someone, the, uh, help, might have put the pages in the trash, you know, tidying up. Maybe there is a bin I could look in?"

Though O.T. took a step toward the recycling container by the backdoor, she knew Will felt the implication that he should do the looking.

"The wife and I wouldn't be putting guests' papers in the trash I can assure you. Perhaps somebody else thought the papers were theirs."

Charlotte heard a knife edge in Will's voice. She rolled her eyes. "The wife . . . theirs . . ." Only Will could be role dismissive and gender inclusive in the same sentence. She buried a snicker in a dish towel. No doubt Will was wondering why she didn't help him out, but the bright light of the kitchen might make her identity clear, not to mention in front of Will. Not good in his current mood. *Why, he might pop a fist at O.T.!* Not that he was given to violence of any kind—he didn't even fish. But this might bring out some buried male defensive or offensive mechanism even though he knew an outline of her history before they married.

"Charlotte? Can you help the professor out?"

She moved to the pantry door, calling out through the dish towel. "If I find anything, I'll let you know right away."

O.T. must have taken the hint to leave since the dining room door opened and closed. *He must think we're a cold lot,* she thought, staying busy in the pantry for another ten minutes not anxious to discuss the incident with Will.

☙

Bea and Ruth hunkered down in their room finally having time after lunch to delve into Westley's book *The Secret of Silence.*

"I like the title, Ruthie, I have to say."

"Yes, we could give him that." They read side by side, commenting with gestures, exclamations, and notes on a pad. By chapter 4 they were fully engaged.

"You know, there's something off about this book," Bea said.

"Yes, it's quite good, is what."

"Maybe Westley's the type to hide his light under a bowl."

"You always give everyone the benefit of the doubt, Bea. This book just doesn't sound like him at all. Wouldn't he write in phony, private eye language? And the setting is Akron told by someone who knows the place."

"Have you been there?"

"No, but after the first chapter I feel as if I have. Westley would make the setting Miami or Los Angeles, someplace he thought crime-ridden. Didn't you hear him go on about the 'intrinsic consequential value of place'?" Ruth's impression of Westley made Bea laugh.

"He's a—what was that word Mr. Cathcart used in his lodge book entry?"

"Blatherskite, a big talker."

"Yeah, Westley is a blatherskite, not a writer. He didn't write this book." Ruth leaned back in the chair.

"I think we know who did. What we need is proof. Why your hand is shaking, Bea. And you're very pale."

"Maybe I should nap. You go take your little walk. Go."

"I can just sit here—"

"Please." Bea put her feet up and sighed. Telling Ruth about her heart scare would just bring them down, leaving them without a book to show for possibly their last efforts together. If she didn't see it finished, Ruth would follow through. Both their names would be on the cover forever, a kind of immortality for their friendship and their art.

———— · ————

16

Dockside Detectives

Not wanting to miss any part of the lodge grounds, Ruth decided to risk a trip to the dock while Bea napped. The Adamsley daughter was down there already and could assist in case she needed help on the steps. The girl had explained while serving breakfast that her father had vetoed her working in Lake Placid. Instead she was helping at the lodge and taking a poetry writing course online.

Ruth avoided mishap and reached the dock where she put out her hand to the girl. "I'm Ruth. How nice the view is here. I hope I can make it back up."

"I'm Alice. I'll be happy to help you."

What a gem this daughter is, Ruth thought. "Glad you're positive. I won't feel I've seen everything unless I visit the dock too." The bench with a back looked safe enough, so she sat down.

"Definitely. How's the workshop going? Are you writing a book?"

"Well, yes. My friend and I like to write mysteries. Maybe I shouldn't say, but we think we've run into one here." Ruth glanced toward the lodge.

"How exciting! I love mysteries. Am I in it?"

"Perhaps! Especially if you can help us with the plot. Now about Phillip Cathcart who was found dead." She flipped open a small notebook.

"Didn't they say he committed suicide? Or drowned by accident? People go out hiking not knowing about the bogs." Alice pantomimed falling in, complete with a sucking sound. "I felt bad for him."

"Did you know him as a guest?"

Ruth listened as Alice described him as a friendly guest with a habit of talking to himself in his cabin. But he was nice to everyone even though he often took his dinner plate to his cabin. Her dad said this wasn't "in the spirit of Blackbird," imitating Will so clearly Ruth laughed. Her mom said that writers need space and he could eat there if he wanted to. Alice tipped her head back and forth reporting the conversation. Apparently, it was a running argument.

"I'd say space is something a person can get a lot of up here." Ruth gestured to the woods.

"You'd think, but no. I can't wait to get out." The girl played with the long hair over her ear.

"Out?"

"Where everyone isn't the same. Where you can be you, if you know what I mean. Not just what people tell you to be."

The girl flipped her hair away from her ear. Maybe her new haircut was a first step toward independence. "And where you can figure out what 'you' is?"

Alice smiled and tucked the long locks behind her ear again. Ruth wanted to draw out anything else the girl might have noticed. *Maybe she has a theory about the death*, Ruth speculated. Young people were often intuitive where adults were dismissive.

"So, what's your theory about Mr. Cathcart?" Ruth poised her pencil.

"I think someone wanted to get rid of him."

"No! Why?"

"If he wanted to kill himself here, why not jump off a rocky cliff? There are plenty around. Saying, 'I think I'll kill myself. Oh, here's a bog. Goodbye world.' That doesn't make sense."

"So, you think suicide by bog is out. Your dad says his death was a fishing accident."

"It could be except that place was way off the map. How would Mr. Cathcart get the idea to fish there? And in a bog without open water?"

"Ahh, someone led or sent him there?" Thinking of the guest book entry, Ruth saw a door open for a disaster.

"Right! No one else believed my theory because why would anyone want him offed? He was just a plain old guest here and very nice." Alice looked glum then brightened up. "Does this give you ideas for your book?"

"You're a sleuth at heart. A motive for someone arranging his death would be helpful to flesh out the theory. Let me know if you think of anything else."

"I have an idea now. Tonight is game night. Dad would never drop Thursday game night even for a writing workshop."

"At last! Cards?"

"Hearts, UNO, or dice games like Parcheesi. And I'll get out the Ouija board and the Magic 8-Ball. We can ask about a motive. Not that I believe that stuff."

Alice bounded up the steps, then came back to offer a hand to Ruth.

———•———

17

Rosemary Chicken, Part II

Dinner was a success. Cinny thought the main dish presentation was like a magazine picture only better, as the scent of rosemary rose when Will carved slices that proved juicy with a lemony tang. Compliments were so genuine that he brought his wife out for applause after dessert, underscoring again the oddity of their being coupled. Maybe his warmth made up for her reticence and chill.

Worry over the arrival of the editor at the back of her mind, Cinny marched everyone to the library for some revision time. If nothing from the writers was impressive enough to take to New York, her efforts could be criticized by both writers and editor. Limp results would be a reflection not only on the mentors but also on the week-long program as a whole. A mediocre evaluation could ruin a plan she had devised. On the phone Mina pointed out that the sponsoring organization could be her future employer. Two English major friends were now event organizers. How much better to plan for events involving travel and the arts than pitching tool shows in Waukegan. Another MFA even parked cars at LAX, the closest he could get to Hollywood so far.

She was determined to wring out some excellence. Before she could focus on readers for the evening, someone asked

O.T. if he had children. That he and Lydia had been married hadn't come to light yet for the writers. This reveal could wreck her plans for an evening of serious revision.

O.T. beamed. "Yes, Luella Larkin and I have a daughter."

"Oh, show us a photo!" Millicent said. "Is she in high school?"

O.T. scrolled to find several photos on his phone that he passed around to surprised "ohs" and a "what a sweetie." They had not expected a toddler. Finally, he clarified. "Luella Larkin and I have been, ah, a couple for five years. Perhaps you know of her books? Romance genre."

Several had read her books, describing them as "so refreshing." Listening to them talk about titles they liked, Cinny realized that Larkin would have been a better fit for the group. Catching O.T.'s eye, she could tell they shared the same thought.

"Just one child? Perhaps more will come, man," Westley said, dumping a silence on the group until a few more questions blossomed about the little girl. O.T. described her, looking happier than he had been all week.

"But you do have sons, too, O.T.," Lydia said.

Cinny heard the slight reproach in Lydia's tone so she jumped up. "Okay, let's get out your—" But Lydia cut her off.

"Actually, O.T. and I share sons. I'd love to show them off." Babble erupted.

"My goodness!"

"Of course, I read he had been married before."

"Was that in his bio?"

"Or hers?"

"Imagine being here together!"

The women chattered as if O.T. and Lydia were deaf until Sarah spoke for everyone. "This is a lesson for all of us on equanimity. How lovely."

"The divorce was years ago," Lydia said and shrugged.

But they still couldn't get to the revisions because Lydia pulled out an album showing the boys from their first day of school, to Eagle Scouts, to college graduation, and ending with the present, the boys, now young men, posing in suits. The writers gabbed on, pondering who the sons favored and their whereabouts. Cinny gave up on the editing.

"And how about all of you? Let's see some photos." Lydia addressed everyone.

Millicent had a photo book, and Sarah got several snapshots from her purse as well as her phone. *Would these parents ever stop?* Cinny wondered as she thumbed her phone to find amusing poses with her kitty.

Charlotte was taking advantage of Lydia's invitation that she join the group in the evenings, and she showed interest in all the photos. According to Lydia, the woman did some writing herself. Again, the thought came to Cinny: *Something is wrong with this picture.* She couldn't put her finger on it, and she was pretty good with observation and character, a compliment O.T. had issued often. This innkeeper seemed mismatched with her environment. Setting should complement the characters, or bring out something, or even hide something.

About to ask Sarah to read her efforts of the day, Cinny saw O.T. gesture for her to follow him to the hallway. *Now what? A reprimand?*

"Listen, we have a problem." He whispered and took a quick vape.

"About the writing quality? It sucks."

"What? Never mind that. The last chapter of my manuscript has disappeared."

"Those pages with all the marginal notes?"

"And the longhand pages too."

She led him to the dining room and like a prosecutor walked him through a timeline of his whereabouts and the disappearance. His hangdog expression was pathetic.

She tried to take his hand. "Want me to go through your room and papers again?" No doubt she would find them under a pile of socks, making him rely even more on her skills and perhaps then he would . . .

He put his hands in his pockets.

"I already did that, and Lydia looked too"—*oh, doesn't that just figure?*—"And I asked the innkeepers and opened the trash bin." He went on and on about all the looking he had done—*i.e., everyone else had done.* She could see the implications before he reached the end of his rant. Without the notes and pages, the shining final chapter, the manuscript to show Zenobia Daly would not be complete.

"So, uh, uh, Cynthia, I think someone picked them up by mistake," he said, then added dropping his voice, "or stole them."

Her mind ran ahead of his speculations. Did he think she might hold his pages for the ransom of reading her manuscript? Her desperation for his help was getting near that level, she had to admit. Theft seemed highly unlikely but was the sort of value he might assume for his pages.

"So, my trusted assistant," his hand on her shoulder felt warm and needy, "I want you to mention this casually. See if we can sniff out anything. After all, maybe one of the ladies or that one guy put them in their bag, pocketbook, or somewhere by accident."

"Okay, but I think tonight we should concentrate on quality revision. We'll be using the guided critique method. It's Sarah's turn to read tonight."

"Which one is that again?"

She reminded him Sarah was the most enthusiastic reader of his book. He brightened. Then she reviewed the evening's activities. Sarah would read, everyone would ask neutral questions and ask her if she wished to hear opinions or suggestions. She fluttered a page in front of him showing the guided response exercise. He nodded, then stepped out to the porch where he scrunched into a tall Adirondack rocker to vape before stomping down to the dock, leaving her to guide the revision session.

Returning to her writers, Cinny was glad to find the photos were put away, and Sarah and Millicent were ready with pages. Sarah's revision of her first black suit story now included other notable outfits and their significance. Millicent used her Paris recollections to create a short story about a Parisian affair.

"Just excellent!" Cinny led the group in clapping after they offered worthwhile suggestions. "Anything to add, O.T.? You missed a fine critique session already." He had just now reappeared.

"Great! Good going! Nothing more from me. Can I have a word with you?" His tone went from peppy to urgent. He gestured to the porch. "Just ask the group about the pages, will you? Some of them look dotty."

Cinny then concluded her pep talk on revision with his request. "When you take these great suggestions back to your rooms, please check through your notebooks and workshop materials for papers that may be Professor O.T.'s. Pages he was working on yesterday afternoon are missing or misplaced."

A flurry of questions followed about his whereabouts, what the pages looked like, what was on them, and where he had already looked. The women knew how to interrogate the boy whose cat ate his homework. Cinny was amused.

"And those pages are your only copy?" Westley said. "How terrible!" His hand traveled to his heart.

"The whole file is online, of course, but not my little editing scribbles. So, if any of you," O.T. stared at the big bag Bea hauled around, "have ideas or find the pages, I'd appreciate having them back."

Cinny knew it smarted to be so casual about this catastrophe. To encourage an embarrassed culprit, she added, "You could just give them to me, or slide them under my door."

Lydia stood up. "In addition to O.T.'s appreciation, we'll give a prize for their return. Check through your stuff. The pages could easily be mixed in."

Cinny wished she had thought of a prize. Inspired by the editing session, the writers might turn dross into gold, or at least silver plate, she hoped. She watched as they began making cross-outs and scribbles on their drafts. O.T., of course, had vanished.

The writers being occupied, Cinny decided to step away for a few minutes and call Mina. "I'm getting a little desperate. O.T. still hasn't looked at my manuscript."

"Is he showering attention on his ex, or LOL, a cougar writer?"

"To tell you the truth, we're pretty busy—the writers are revising and finally putting out stuff with potential. Even O.T. is holding little conferences. I don't think he's had a lot of time for romance."

"Mmm-hmm."

"But get this, some of his manuscript pages disappeared."

"You mean like lost? Stolen?"

"He says they disappeared while he was getting a cup of coffee. Now he won't have a full manuscript for Zenobia."

"You didn't—"

"Of course not!"

"Just thinking that's a way to have your manuscript proposal stand out. Maybe someone else got that idea too."

"Maybe."

"It could be. Is anyone, you know, angry with him? Or psychotic? Jealous?"

"The woman who runs the lodge is kind of standoffish. A holier-than-thou type."

"What's her mojo? Sexy? Outdoorsy type? Career woman somewhere else?"

"A closet writer according to O.T.'s ex."

"There you go! She's jealous of you running the seminar. She's getting in the way of your success."

"Possibly. There's definitely something going on."

Millicent holding out her notebook cut off more speculation and they disconnected.

———·———

18

O.T.'s Peek through the Looking-Glass

Prepping the fireplace in the library with paper and wood was Alice's job. For many guests a wood fire was a novelty and felt good in the summer chill that was not unusual in the mountains. She dumped the kindling on the hearth, surprised to find paper already in the fireplace, too much paper, enough for a bonfire. She pulled out some sheets, curious about someone else's failed literary efforts. Then she noticed the running head: Bookman. Though kind of snooping, but he had meant to throw them away, she started reading. Then—

Oh my God! These could be the missing pages that she had heard about earlier. Her parents were unhappy that the lead mentor had implied that their lodge supervision was slipshod.

"Mom!" Alice raced to her mother's office and handed over the pages. Her mother wanted more details about the discovery.

"There wasn't anyone in the library or anything else lying around. Someone put the pages in the fireplace for burning but didn't crinkle them very much."

As her mother nodded agreement, Alice looked out the window. "Oh! Dr. Bookman's down on the dock. I'm going to take them down there now."

"I can do—" she heard her mom say, but the mission was hers.

Alice trotted down the steps to the dock waving the pages. "Dr. Bookman! Are these what you were looking for?"

She put them in his hands.

"Yes, these are the missing ones. Where were they?"

He was so thankful. She gave him a full account of her chore involving the library fireplace, entering the room, and unloading the kindling to find paper already in the fireplace. Though they debated how or why the pages were there, his relief at getting them back overshadowed any interest in the culprit or mismanagement that had landed them there. His manner invited further friendliness, so she decided she could linger.

"My mom said you're married to Luella Larkin. I've read a couple of her books. I like that everything turns out happily in the end, though I'm not really into the romance genre, per se." He shouldn't think she was an airhead.

"Me either." They had a laugh while admitting this shared attitude.

"You have to fake interest, then? Oh, that's not the right word." *I am an airhead.* She got up to leave, but he didn't seem insulted.

"You mean it's difficult to praise her books without being disingenuous?"

"Yeah, exactly." He was listening carefully, as if this conversation mattered. "To be honest, Dr. Bookman, I haven't read your books. One is really famous though, my mom said."

"You're about the right age to appreciate it."

"I'll be nineteen next month. I go to the University at Albany." Naming the college gave her sophistication. Most graduates from her high school who enrolled in college went to local campuses.

"An excellent school. And what are you studying?"

"I'm majoring in 'undecided' so far. My dad says to study something with 'money in it at the end.'" She used air quotes. "But I'm thinking of English."

"There's no guarantee of money there." Dr. Bookman pressed his lips together to look stern, then laughed.

"My mom found that out. She writes stories, articles, a book once, and even when they don't all sell, she keeps going." Maybe she shouldn't have revealed this pursuit, but she admired her mom's perseverance, and he should understand they weren't hillbillies.

"In fact, she has an MFA from the University of Michigan." She knew this was an impressive credential.

"Ann Arbor?"

Alice nodded. He seemed so surprised, even kind of jolted, so she added, "She's really smart."

Maybe she was bothering him, babbling about her family, because he kept looking up at the lodge.

She got to the steps and had waved goodbye when he stopped her. "Don't forget, there's a reward for finding these pages. Be sure to tell my assistant you're the winner."

"I will."

She jogged up the steps thinking that unlike some other profs she had encountered last year, he was very personable.

———— • ————

19

Game Time

Millicent searched her closet for one of her new outfits for the evening's games. *Why not dress up?* She rejected a sailor-style top. Navy and white was much more suited to the Cape, if her sister invited her this year. Instead, in the spirit of decadence, she chose maroon, velvety leisure wear. Sarah never changed her outfit from morning to night, but wardrobe was part of vacation fun in Millicent's crowd.

In terms of her choice of workshops, this one was going quite well. She would have some pretty good story pieces and photos to show friends at home. Though the companions weren't fascinatingly eccentric or wealthy, she liked them well enough, especially the innkeeper, Will, who looked like the men in the outfitter catalog, sturdy and sexy. Apparently, he wasn't the type to play around—he had taken up none of her overtures.

Westley was a different story. She hadn't spent the night in his cabin yet, but they had watched the sunset and his hand wandered. When he stopped by to pick her up for game night, she admired his gold ascot and quickly found a matching scarf.

"This should be fun," Millicent said. "Something different and a break from my draft." She had left her notebook out on the table as evidence.

"Ah, yes, the story of your family's early years?"

"I think my son might find it interesting, especially about my grandmother's arrival on Ellis Island."

"One can always hope." He glanced at the notebook. "But remember some personal episodes are best kept out of the light."

This remark was a little off-putting, so Millicent changed the subject. "We should be on our way, I guess."

"After you, milady." Westley's gentlemanly manners were refreshing.

🖋

Glad to have no evening responsibilities, Cinny was in the mood for games, as were the writers, who had dug in at her dialogue clinic that afternoon. Conversation between story characters had gone from robotic to real. Lydia complimented her expertise so sincerely that she felt revived to work on her own manuscript. O.T. had been absent though she had seen him sprint up from the dock and pass through the lodge.

Game night was Will's gig apparently. He and Alice led rounds of Parcheesi and UNO, Will sprinkling in historic tidbits about the lodge. The evening was interesting and fun. At nine when Alice asked whether they wanted to get out the Ouija board and Magic 8-Ball, her father recounted how in the old days spiritualists entertained at the great camps.

"Then we must try to reach the spirits too." Bea was always ready for anything, Cinny had noticed.

After her father excused himself, Alice flipped off the overhead lights and turned on two sconces with arms made of antlers. The small bulbs cast a dim glow.

"These are original, though they used to be oil. Kind of creepy, right?" She gestured for them to draw in close around one table then set the Magic 8-Ball in front of Sarah.

"You want to start us off?"

Sarah hefted the black ball and shared how her daughters had dropped one on the hall floor, splashing the dark liquid onto the carpet in the living room. "If I could have them as little girls again for a week, they could drop ten Magic 8-Balls. I wouldn't care a bit."

Cinny was surprised how quickly the other mothers agreed as Sarah massaged the ball.

"Will it rain tomorrow?" She turned the ball to watch the answer float up. "'Don't count on it.' Amazing! Absolutely true. The forecast is only 10 percent rain!" Everyone clapped.

Sarah handed the toy to Millicent whose scarf matched Westley's. *On purpose?* Cinny pondered this coincidence.

Millicent rocked the ball in several circles. She closed her eyes saying, "Is my latest story good?"

Murmurs followed about Millicent's bravery, and all offered hopes that the spirits were gentle critics. Cinny leaned in to see whether the answer from the Beyond matched her appraisal. The message under the inky liquid read, "Don't count on it."

Millicent was a good sport and laughed, saying the ball was just stuck in a rut, and passed it to Ruth.

"You people are taxing the magic. I'll ask an easy one. 'Do I look fat in my bathing suit?'"

These women know how to have a good time. Cinny watched Ruth give the ball a kiss and a spin. She read, "My sources say No."

Everyone cheered, and Ruth added, "There, now what do you think about the prediction accuracy?"

"Don't answer, people!" Bea yelped waving her hands.

Alice took a turn asking about whether she would get an A in her summer poetry course. "Better not tell you now," she read.

"That's to make sure you keep working hard." O.T. rambled in and offered this logic. Cinny moved a chair into the circle next to her.

Lydia asked whether brussels sprouts were her favorite vegetable, getting the response, "Most likely." She agreed a taste for sprouts was likely but not true.

O.T. took the ball from her. He sent Lydia a look and asked whether his editor would like his latest draft. "Very doubtful."

Everyone assured him the ball's literary taste was probably "pedestrian," but Lydia poked him, saying the historic lodge might be the place to find the magic he needed.

At her turn Cinny asked if she should dye her hair black. "Most assuredly!"

Alice offered her a DIY kit she had in her room left over from Halloween.

"Oh ho, are we changing from workshop to spa?" O.T. said. His enthusiasm seemed overplayed to Cinny. *He's on something.*

Westley looked peeved at this lowbrow entertainment, and when Millicent put the ball in his hand, he passed it on.

Bea asked whether there would be any surprises at the end of the week. The answer "Better not tell you now" brought out hoots all around.

Lydia said, "Obviously, the genie wants to keep our writing muses on task."

"Or prepare us for the letdown!" Sarah added.

Cinny felt she should take charge at this point since the evening was winding down and again complimented their day's revision efforts.

❧

O.T stepped out for a surreptitious vape, hoping to quiet the tremor in his hands. On the dock earlier, like a report from the Magic 8-Ball, the name "Carly" had floated into his consciousness. *No wonder the girl's mother looked familiar!* They had known each other well indeed.

Since his realization, he had alternated between hiding out and roaming around looking for an opening to confirm Carly's identity and atone for not recognizing her. Perhaps she would come back to the dining room after the games to straighten up. He pondered various outcomes.

Before anyone could make a move for the cabins, Bea said, "The spirits are warmed up now. Let's do the Ouija board."

Chairs were drawn in closer still as Alice got out an old fashioned planchette and board.

Westley stood to leave, but Ruth said, "Oh, do stay. We need more men to protect us. Look how spooky the night's getting. The clouds have covered the moon."

Millicent gave him a raised eyebrow and smile and took his hand. Ruth put her fingers on the planchette joined by Alice and Millicent. Bea felt her senses sharpen on hearing the sighing of limbs and leaves above the lake.

Alice said, "Let's start with something easy. 'What is my cat's name?'"

Nothing happened at first. Just as Millicent said the spirits were tired of them all, the planchette skidded over letters E-L-E-Y and stopped.

"My cat's name is Ellie, so that's almost right."

"Yes, a phonetic spelling," Lydia said.

Cinny took Millicent's place on the planchette. "Where did I lose my phone?"

Bea glanced at Ruth. The planchette slid not hovering on any letters, finally hovering on L after skimming over B and A.

"Ball? I haven't been to any balls."

"How about a ballgame?" O.T. said from the doorway. Cinny shook her head at his question.

"Mall, have you been to a mall?" Alice said.

"Oh, yeah! The same week my phone went missing."

"So psychic!" Millicent whispered drawing closer to Westley. Bea saw him flinch when she gripped his hand with both of hers.

Ruth gestured and she and Bea replaced Cinny and Alice on the planchette. Bea spoke very gently. "Does someone from Beyond want to contact us?"

The wind was growing in strength, requiring they speak up over the board. Bea felt the planchette move to "Yes" immediately and rest there.

Westley pulled his hand from Millicent.

"Who?"

Bea felt Ruth nudge her foot, and they leaned in closer. The planchette spun from letter to letter.

C-A-T—

Westley changed position so quickly his chair nearly tipped over.

"There are lots of cats over the Rainbow Bridge," Millicent was saying as the planchette took off again.

H-C-A-R-T

"Cathcart, the dead guest! What does he want to tell us?" Alice whispered.

"That you all are wasting a good evening. Your spirit is a phony." Westley's comment was strident and the planchette skidded on the board.

"Whatever!" Millicent sent a playful glance at Westley, then added, "Let's keep going anyway."

The planchette dithered here and there resting on M-U-R-D and then nothing after thunder made everyone jump. Bea put her hands in her lap when Ruth said, "That was a message: 'Go to bed!'"

Bea handed the planchette to Alice who clearly had something to say to them, but Ruth was heading toward the door. The rest of the party broke up too. O.T. announced he was going to call home, another evasion of Cinny, no doubt. *That young woman shouldn't waste time on him*, Bea thought. Millicent kept her arm through Westley's, perhaps to guide them toward his cabin.

Good luck with that one, Bea thought as she followed Ruth toward their cabin.

———— • ————

20

Rosemary Chicken, Part III

Wʜᴇɴ ɢᴀᴍᴇ ɴɪɢʜᴛ ꜰɪɴᴀʟʟʏ ᴇɴᴅᴇᴅ, Charlotte left her office to turn off the lights in the dining room. A noise came from the kitchen. *A guest hoping for tea and toast?* Will might be happy to oblige, but she wasn't.

She slid into the cranny between the chimney and buffet, inexcusable to hide from a guest, but it was after eleven. Instead of opening quickly, the door swung bit by bit as someone carefully surveyed the dining room. She drew back even further.

O.T. sidled in.

It was the moment she'd been waiting for. Time together alone!

But if she stepped out or spoke, she would look as if she had been waiting to pounce, like Jack Nicholson in *The Shining*. Why, O.T. might cry out, alerting Will or Alice.

Maybe he's looking for me. The idea came and went. *More likely the bottle of wine from dinner.*

Then he dithered around the buffet, so close that a musky scent floated to her. *English Leather. Still.* As her self-control was about to fail, he opened her lodge notebook lying on the table. He riffled the pages and laid something inside, then dashed up the stairs without looking back just as she stepped out. In her notebook she found a tiny nosegay of rosemary, apparently pilfered from sprigs in the kitchen.

"Rosemary, that's for remembrance." Charlotte spoke the lines from *Hamlet* as she picked up the nosegay. *A token instead of speaking to me.* She looked toward the stairs. *So like him.*

It was the recognition she had hoped for, yet her next move was unclear. Throw it out, go up to his room, show it to Will? Her nightly last look at the lake might help her decide, so she went to the dock. A wind rippled the water, driving the canoes to uneasily clash against each other. Charlotte shivered, thinking it might be prophetic of Will's reaction to finding out O.T.'s relationship to her and Alice. As much as O.T.'s failure to remember her had been demoralizing, her failure to alert Will of this coincidental arrival loomed larger.

Before tossing the leaves into the water, Charlotte breathed deeply into the nosegay. The musk of English Leather remained and sent an arrow of delight. *Remembrance!* She stood transfixed as the waterlogged nosegay sank, perhaps as gently as Ophelia. Drowning was a way out of this fiasco Charlotte hoped wouldn't be necessary.

———•———

21

A Reading in New York

DURING GAME NIGHT AT BLACKBIRD LODGE, in New York City, Netta Simpson set aside the slush pile to prepare for the writing workshop. She settled on her Murphy bed with O.T.'s books, *Drowning in Freedom*, his lauded first novel, and *Caught in the Act*, his recent book, now eight years old. She also had *In Her Element*, a biography about a minor female poet by Lydia Beauvais Galesberg, and a book by Luella Larkin, *Mountain Laurel*.

She stared at the author photo of Bookman on his first novel's cover, his eyes soft and compelling. She scanned the cover blurbs: "Moves like a freight train through the reader's psyche . . . masterful descriptive powers." "Updike and Dylan combined . . . the voice of a young America coming into its own."

Before she dove in, Netta looked at a review of the more recent novel: "Author of *Drowning in Freedom* continues his descriptive traditions in *Caught in the Act* . . . many introspective musings . . . revisits previous themes." She was surprised by the less-than-stellar endorsements. She appraised the jacket photo, a man trying too hard in a black turtleneck, a few lines around the eyes, though still good-looking.

She turned over Galesberg's book: "Entertaining and readable . . . brings to life an overlooked and talented poet . . .

scholarly flair." Though Netta expected the usual artiste photo favored for middle-aged women on book jackets, Lydia Galesberg had a whimsical smile and the good looks of a happy woman. Her bio noted where she taught and said she hiked with her dog. Having read that they had been married, she held the two photos, O.T. and Lydia, together. No, they did not look compatible now, if they ever were. Did this explain why they were willing to appear together at this workshop?

She flipped over *Mountain Laurel* to read the back cover: "A call for help sends Laurel McLayre to the remote estate of her estranged father where the reclusive gardener . . ." A stamp-sized author photo showed quite a young woman.

At midnight Netta made herself put down *Drowning in Freedom.* The book was everything the cover promised and more. Even twenty years off, the novel spoke magically in the voices of her own generation! It was a terrific book. She started *Caught in the Act,* just to get the flavor of his most current book, but by one thirty, she set it aside. It was not a terrific book, good, but not terrific.

As she settled in bed, a thought so startling came to her that she sat up and hit her head on the reading light. *O.T. Bookman's next book could be my killer find!* A coup like that would advance her title to editor.

Netta considered some scenarios. Perhaps he was only a one-book wonder. On the other hand, maybe he was just coming into his full power. Maybe his next project would be seminal—she had read he was working on a new book. *What a team we could be.* "My heartfelt thanks to Netta, my editor, without whose help . . . her insightful editing, right-on-target instincts, and feel for great literature . . . this book wouldn't have won the Pulitzer Prize." *Well!* The book's dedication would be a veiled reference to their relationship, perhaps a line from an obscure poem they both loved. Perhaps they would be lovers. No, that would be tacky and complicated. *Besides, he's kind of old.*

As Netta drifted off, she replayed the scripts over and over with a further twist. Not only would she be his editor, but he also would inspire her own best writing. The symbiotic relationship would lead them both to the *New York Times* best-seller list.

Early Saturday morning she would drive north in her rented Kia. O.T. Bookman didn't know what good fortune was coming his way.

———— • ————

22

— FRIDAY —

Artful Displays, Museum and Otherwise

O.T. WAS SURPRISED TO BE WIDE AWAKE at dawn on Friday, but he restrained himself from getting up. He hadn't felt this animated in months, as if he could knock out a rewrite of the final chapters. He should go down to the porch, no, sit at his table by the window and get busy. Whether anticipation or dread was firing his synapses, it didn't matter. He just felt fully alive, but he lay abed ten minutes more, picturing what might be going on elsewhere in the lodge.

The inn mistress's identity had burst on him yesterday afternoon. Unbelievably, for four days he been oblivious to the parallel universe playing out in the lodge. He relived the theatrical moment of recognition on the dock.

The lodge daughter skipped down the steps with his wrinkled pages. He thanked her, and during a pleasant chat, her profile, expressive gestures, and wit struck him as familiar. As the girl talked about how her mother had an MFA, the features assembled into a figure. He had nearly blacked out, then charged up the steps looking for someone who must surely be her mother. His Carly!

Back in his room he had swallowed two Xanax before assessing the potential for damage—or adventure. *Who knows what in the lodge?* He had ticked off what he knew. He and Carly had altered their names, she to a longer form and he to an abbreviated one. Surely, she would have known he was coming after receiving the workshop details. Feeling heart-attack-ish, he had also gulped two aspirin while weighing chances for other recognitions and their results.

Did Lydia know who Carly-Charlotte was? Probably not. She would have already held him accountable for this disastrous ménage à trois.

Cinny? Would she guess? He had avoided her advances and intimacies of various kinds, thank God, so she should have no suspicions or recriminations.

Finally, he had come up against the most troubling thought: *Had Carly, ah Charlotte, assumed all week I was pretending I didn't know her?* That made him a terrible cad . . . or maybe, heroic? Her husband was an imposing guy, not the type to welcome his wife's old—*not old, but former*—lover. *No doubt this was why Carly didn't greet me warmly the first day.*

Before turning in last night, he had lit on the idea of leaving her the rosemary.

As he lay under his twisted sheet, various next moves came to him, some cautious, some salacious. *It's up to her now. The next move should be hers,* he decided. Then he flung himself out of bed and into the new day.

The sunshine after a gloomy Thursday seemed like a good omen. He showered, put on a blue linen shirt, applied a dash of aftershave, and took the stairs two at a time. On the slightest signal, he would draw his Carly into a corner, cup her familiar face in his hands, and say how he had missed her all these years.

Though he usually had just coffee and a bagel, to stay longer in the dining room he ate eggs, bacon, and pancakes. He sympathized at length over the challenges of publishing a first book and agreed when Lydia and Cinny insisted he accompany the writers on a morning outing. Then he toured the lodge and grounds, including the dock. Carly-Charlotte was nowhere in sight.

Cinny had awoken in a good mood because today they would get out of the woods. Though the online blurb suggested the museum was dedicated to the history and culture of the area—and she had had enough local color related to the great camps, edible plants, etc.—the museum promised memorabilia from regional writers. Best of all, the outing required nothing from her.

Charlotte had been awake nearly until dawn. Though the nosegay was a validation of the past, the tiny gift was a cumbersome bundle now between her and Will, a parcel she shouldn't—or maybe should—unwrap for all their sakes. Had this been a romance novel, her character would have been drawn to the porch where her former lover waited to embrace her. In fact, she was a little afraid Otis-O.T. might set up such a scene, or in a moment of weakness, she might substitute an unhinged encounter for the mature one she ought to have. Therefore, at seven she went directly to the kitchen to make the box lunches for the day trip and stayed there while Will cooked and set out breakfast.

"People always like the museum, especially the older set," Will said as she packaged oatmeal cookies.

"What?" Ordinary conversation was challenging when another potential dialogue was running in her head.

"I said, the writers will like the museum and you'll get some time off." He flooded yellow hollandaise sauce on eggs, ham, and English muffins. Charlotte admired his perfect eggs and slid one on a plate. With a flourish he added a dollop more sauce for her. His consideration felt undeserved.

"Oh, the museum. I've toured too often this summer, especially the taxidermy exhibit. Those dead rabbits arranged into scenes. It's pathetic," she said.

"Taxidermy is regional history whether we like it or not."

"So why not display some dead TB patients? They're part of our history too."

"You are in a mood." He put the eggs on platters, kissed her on the top of her head, and carried the plates into the dining room.

"I'll be back about two." The door had already swung shut. Maybe he had heard, maybe not, but he knew the museum routine.

Over the clatter of coffee cups and forks, Charlotte could hear O.T. being friendly in a condescending way. He would likely drive his own car or wiggle out of the museum trip. *Reunion will have to wait,* she concluded.

Half an hour later Charlotte pulled the van up the gravel drive for her group. She chatted freely once she saw O.T. was not in the lineup of museumgoers. Cinny had Bea, Ruth, Sarah, Millicent, and Westley in tow.

"We're still so interested in that disappearance of Mr. Cathcart, Charlotte," Bea said after she settled her big bag on the seat.

"The police think the death was an accidental drowning." In the rearview mirror Charlotte saw rapt faces at her comment.

"What's your personal theory?" Bea leaned toward her. "Did he seem involved in something, say, shady?"

"Women are more intuitive. What do you think?" Ruth added. Charlotte could see her rummaging in her pocket and taking out a notebook.

"He really didn't seem like the type for shady activities. Unless you call writing a book shady." Everyone laughed in camaraderie.

"But why would a man set out to fish in a bog where there is no open water?" Ruth said, and Bea leaned over the seat again with a follow-up.

"And why was there no manuscript in his cabin if he was working on one?"

"He must have had it with him." Westley sounded as if this were the definitive answer. Millicent followed him with the conclusion, "And it sank."

"More likely," Sarah said, "he threw the whole thing out. I've ripped up a notebook's worth of paper so far this week." Charlotte saw her mimic a violent disposal in the rearview mirror.

"Well, maybe we can unravel the mystery more with the locals." Bea passed around a tin of mints and waved it over the driver's seat. "Your Alice has an interesting theory."

Reference to Alice startled Charlotte out of a daydream involving O.T. and a bed of springy moss. Her daughter's name was a reminder to stick to the reasonable discussion with O.T. that she had scripted.

Arrival at the museum stirred her passengers to action. Cinny helped Bea out of the van, distributed museum tickets, and put the sack lunches on a picnic table. With hours to fill Charlotte left the van in the parking lot and decided on a ramble, stopping first at the Arts & Crafts Cottage. She hadn't been in lately to look at local arts like balsam sachets and watercolors of mountain sunsets, as well as garnet jewelry.

"Could I show you something?" A saleswoman, who assumed she was a tourist, explained that most garnets from Adirondack mines went into sandpaper, thus the jewelry was a unique souvenir.

"I'm just looking."

"Isn't this one lovely?" From the case the woman handed her a faceted stone caught in a gold twist.

The pendant was so blood red that it felt warm in her palm. "Very beautiful." Charlotte turned over the price tag. "Two hundred dollars?"

"As you can see, very reasonable and set in 14-karat gold." The woman gestured for Charlotte to try on the necklace. "Just let me do the fastener for you. You'll see how nice it drapes."

"Maybe another time." But she didn't move fast enough. The woman closed the clasp around her neck and the stone now nestled below her collarbones.

"Our artist makes very few of each design. This one she calls a love knot. See how the garnet sets in the center twist?"

"Ensnared" might be a better word, Charlotte thought, observing the gold threads crisscrossing the stone. "I'll think about it. Mind if I take a photo?"

"Go right ahead. This piece won't last long, though." The woman held the door open for her with a last encouragement. "The other one like this went a week ago. A tall fellow, pleased he found something special from what he said."

On a nearby bench Charlotte thumbed to the photo. *Yes, definitely.* Only last week she had seen the garnet love knot on Tabby Douglass, whose husband was short and chubby.

So, when O.T.'s Lexus pulled into the museum parking lot, the sensibly mature encounter scene she had assembled evaporated. She waved and accepted his invitation to get in. *Why not?*

He leaned toward her and took her left hand in both of his. "Carly, I just didn't notice it was you at first. You know me, always in my own head." He pressed her fingers to his lips like a supplicant. "Can you ever forgive me?"

She melted inside, the "never, you egomaniac" turned into a compliant, watery yes, until he babbled on.

"You seemed familiar, but I see so many women I couldn't place—"

What a lame excuse! She should have told him how disappointed and angry she had been, but when he reached to touch more of her she said, "Did you keep the couch?"

"What?"

"The saggy one in your office." He didn't smell like English Leather today. Something less erotic.

"Oh, God, that old couch. I gave it to the Alphas, I think." His blue gaze fully rested on her. "Carly, we were so young and full of life."

In his arms over the gearshift, she felt kisses turn from chaste to luscious. When had she last felt this rending want? At last, she pulled away.

"Congratulations on your book. You're famous now."

"Was famous. My second book was a bomb, more or less. Maybe I lacked my muse!" He moved in close again, this time cupping her face and brushing back her hair in a familiar, intimate way. "What happened to us, Carly?"

She was reaching for him, too, when she recognized a component of her disgust with the museum rabbits— something dead rejuvenated and placed in a phony scene. She drew back.

"You had a wife, which we conveniently forgot. One day I saw you playing basketball with your boys." There they were, sons and a dad. "I realized it was time for me to move on."

"Turned out, my wife said it was time for her to move on too. She took the boys with her to Iowa."

How awful. Charlotte couldn't imagine Will moving away with Alice or her taking Alice from Will.

"You moved on. You have a new family." She couldn't entirely tamp down sarcasm, but he must have suffered when he couldn't see his boys often.

Surely, he would ask about her family soon, about Alice, so when he suggested they go for a ride, she agreed.

"You've got quite the place up here. It's fantastic. Tell me how this happened."

She explained how she came east to work and met Will, embellishing only a little her past nineteen years, saying she had written for local publications and intended to write the history of the lodge, an idea that only came to her at that moment. He nodded along, asked about property values, and stopped at a roadside park. She pointed out a trail to the falls, the perfect place for the scene she had promised herself she would evade, but the garnet purchased by the "tall fellow" kept invading her thoughts.

They ambled down the trail.

"Did you know right away it was me who left the rosemary?" His hope was so boyish she laughed.

"Of course. Such a literary thing to do."

"And romantic too?"

He reached for her hand as they followed the soft trail under balsam fir and black birch. His fingers didn't have the substance of Will's, but their familiarity unearthed a younger, competitive self. She couldn't let his *Hamlet* reference rest.

"Romantic? Let's review the scene. Ophelia used rosemary as a plea to her brother for remembrance. Next she drowns herself."

"No, no, not suicide!" Like old times, he took the bait and fit his arm over her shoulders. "You've forgotten. The grave diggers conclude the water met the lady, not that the lady met the water."

"Ah, yes, thus she could be buried in consecrated ground. Still, this is not a romantic allusion." She knew her literary tease was only a weak cover of a literal one, but still her better judgment ruled. She moved away from his arm.

At the falls, cardinal flowers as bright as garnets grew in the open ground. O.T. suggested they sit on a large rock and picked several flower stalks.

"There's a new interpretation I heard from students. You'll like it."

"Tell me."

"Ophelia pregnant by Hamlet courageously chose to end her life, singing and sinking covered in wildflowers." He playacted a dive into the stream clutching the stalks to his chest. This was the old beguiling Otis, but she ducked when he pressed the red blossoms to her face.

"Unlike Ophelia I'm not ready to die. Cardinal flower is poisonous." She laid the stems aside. "Where's the textual evidence? No way would Ophelia have drowned herself from shame or to save reputations, if pregnant. Did you give someone an A for that idea? How would this be courageous? Are you not woke?"

He laughed and massaged her thigh. "That's my old Carly, a spitfire. Listen to us now. Isn't this where we left off years ago, arguing about literature?" He was leaning back lazily twirling a flower stem.

Though the timing was perfect to tell him about Alice— like an act four or the peak of the story arc—introducing her merely as anecdotal evidence would be a betrayal of the last nineteen years with Will.

"These analyses seem trivial now, Otis. Back then I thought literature was the world." It seemed incredible that this sort of erudite debating had been enough for her when there was so much else to explore. Here was the waterfall reduced from cascade to trickle midsummer and the clumps of cardinal flowers with their poison more interesting and as fully symbolic as a poem, lovely and complex both.

"Carly, you haven't changed a bit. You're so perceptive, still my best muse." He put his arm around her again trying to move closer. "Maybe it's not too late for us?"

Alice had wondered what living with her biological father would have been like. It was pretty obvious. O.T. would always be ready for a fling for old time's sake or a novelty anytime.

"Don't hide up here." He gave her a long look and stepped back when she said nothing. "Whatever happened to that book you were writing?"

Scenes near the end that evaded her became very clear right then. The protagonist wasn't the young woman character at all but her mother. A revision began to take shape. "I'm almost finished."

"Ah, good for you." He patted her thigh. "Say, you don't think you'd be willing to go through my last chapter? You know, just check for wordiness or point-of-view shifts?"

Charlotte removed his hand. "You haven't changed a bit either, Otis, even with a new name. Thank you for the rosemary nosegay. Very clever."

She gave him a chaste kiss and headed along the path back to the car taking in only phrases as he trotted behind her. "I'm really sorry about . . . You look terrific . . . Your husband seems nice . . . Pretty daughter."

They drove back to her van in silence.

☙

Back at the lodge, the writers thanked Charlotte for the day out. The museum had pleased them. Opinions varied on the taxidermy exhibit, but everyone liked the displays about local writers and painters. Charlotte wished the writers a "happy nap" and went to her office directly from parking the van.

Well, that's that. Charlotte expected to feel more as she sat at her desk. O.T. had wanted to link up after recognizing her and his desire felt genuine. And now that her ego was repaired, she could focus fully on her lack of honesty with Will. The week was nearly over. Maybe she should wait until everyone had gone before explaining. Or not tell him at all. Was honesty always the best policy if someone would be hurt?

She turned on her computer and visited the website for Arts & Crafts Cottage. As she scrolled through the jewelry, Alice popped in.

"Online shopping? Let's see." Charlotte felt the delicious weight of her daughter leaning on her shoulder. "That's like the one that Tabby Douglass had. Pretty, if you like red stones."

"Just like hers?"

"Absolutely. I talked to her about it.

"What'd she say?" Charlotte kept her tone light.

"The necklace was a gift or something. You should have a garnet if you like them. Put that on your birthday list. Bye! Gotta go make a call." Alice blew a kiss at the door.

Will came in as she left. Charlotte waited a few seconds before closing the web page. He said nothing though he had to have seen the image.

"How was the day? Did you avoid the taxidermy?" He massaged her shoulders briefly.

She wished she were brave enough to break into their shared bubble of nondisclosure.

"I shopped around instead and went for a ride." She wished he would ask with whom but wondering about a male companion wouldn't occur to him. "Arts & Crafts Cottage has some nice garnet pieces. They sell well apparently. Like the one Tabby Douglass wore all the time last week—"

"Time for me to start the potatoes."

He left without another word.

Fine. He wasn't going to talk about it, the something with that woman. If there was nothing, why give her an expensive gift and not tell his wife? If there was something, Tabby had a lot of nerve wearing the garnet openly around the lodge.

Ruth came out of the powder room to find Westley by the row of family portraits on the wall. One took his interest so much that he had lifted the frame off its hook.

"My goodness be careful. That frame might be delicate." She caught a scrim of forced goodwill that covered his displeasure at seeing her.

"Cleveland Whitehead, the last rightful owner." He held the frame next to his head. "Do you see a likeness?"

She stepped back for a better analysis. "Should I?"

"My great-great-uncle."

"Is that so?" She clapped a hand to her cheek and thought, *Red alert.* "How fascinating!"

"He has a widow's peak." Westley pointed to his own hairline. "A family trait through the generations." He lowered his forehead to show the line.

"Right, I do see it. A pity you are too young to have ever met him."

"Yes, that's so, but I feel I know him. Like me, he met sad reversals in his lifetime through no fault of his own."

The edge in his voice made Ruth step back as she said, "Ah, 1929. And then Adamsley won the lodge via a wager. Another reversal." She tsked twice.

"A win according to that tale he told." He gestured toward the kitchen.

"A win in legend only?"

"Thievery is the right word."

His grip was so strong on the frame that gilt flakes fell to his trousers as he opened the side door. She tried to step in front of him. "Where are you going with the picture? Perhaps we'd better ask Will."

"My cabin. The picture and cabin both are rightfully mine after all."

Ruth waited until he got to his doorway before rushing at top speed to find Bea.

———— • ————

23

Revelations at Rosco's Open Mic

Though he would as soon stay home, Will geared up for open mic night at Rosco's. He'd go to show respect for the workshop and to please Charlotte. They had attended this Friday event occasionally, but the poems about lost love or rants about the government lacked literary merit in his opinion. Charlotte wrote circles around these turkeys, and he often told her so. Some nights, a musician would inspire wild applause leading to an encore and another pitcher.

The writers piled into the van and acted happy to see that he was the driver, a different audience for their small talk. They let him know Cinny had encouraged two of them to bring poems and that Professors Bookman and Galesberg were going to present readings also.

Will chatted along, thinking the writers' workshop had been an easy week and that the ladies might be ill-prepared for the atmosphere at Rosco's. A banner announcing open mic night drew attention away from the stained siding and logs, but the lineup of road hogs spoke of the patrons. Conversation veered to the menu.

"What do you suggest we order?"

"Do they have a special?"

He figured they wouldn't go wrong choosing the Italian beef or barbecued pork sandwiches.

"I'm sure the local folk will be entertaining." Westley's remark offended Will, as did everything else about the man.

"Why Westley, meeting people is the best part of any vacation," Bea said, with Ruth adding, "As you should know."

Westley hurried off toward the entrance alone. Will doubted the ladies would miss his company.

Sarah and Millicent stood by the van to take in the surroundings. Will heard Sarah say, "One of my daughters had a boyfriend with a motorcycle," before Millicent urged them inside. He hoped the evening didn't turn raucous.

Cinny was last out of the van and paced around, probably looking for Bookman, maybe finally figuring out the guy bailed whenever he could. They both watched as Lydia and Bookman got out of his Lexus. Charlotte had explained they were exes. Will studied the couple and shrugged. Apparently, writer people kept no lasting hard feelings.

☙

Charlotte enjoyed driving to Rosco's with Alice as a passenger, though she was curious why Alice was going along. Still shaken by afternoon discoveries, she had to work at assuming a casual air, doubly challenging when Alice brought up O.T.

"Dr. Bookman would be a cool prof," Alice said.

"What makes you think so?" *What had Alice seen in him?*

"He was really nice when I brought him his pages. I'm supposed to get a prize from Cinny he said."

"How nice."

"I told him I'd read books by Ms. Larkin, but that I hadn't read his book."

"What did he say about that?" Charlotte found a place to park but maneuvered slowly to prolong the conversation.

"Nothing especially, but come to think of it, the book's probably the prize for finding his pages. Have you read it?"

"Only recently for the workshop. It's very—"

Alice flung open the car door. "Gotta go. There're my friends." She rushed off. Charlotte reached over to close the door. Apparently, a mother's appraisal of O.T.'s book was not interesting.

Entering Rosco's, Charlotte worked through the crowded room looking for Will and was relieved to see it was unlikely Alice and O.T. would be close enough for a resemblance to be noticed. Will was already at a table with a pitcher.

"Tonight should have a different flavor, don't you think?" Will said passing her a glass. "Competition from the workshop poets might keep some of the local bards from making it big."

"No one has made it big yet with a start here." She felt herself relaxing in the friendly atmosphere. Everyone's attention would be on the lodge guests, not her family.

"Don't be so sure! Someday people will be saying 'I knew Charlotte Adamsley when she was at Rosco's.'" Will squeezed her hand. "You should read sometime."

"Sometime." She gave him her usual answer.

They looked around, taking in how Rosco's was done up for the occasion. White lights over the square dance floor replaced the disco ball, and chairs and tables had been rearranged. At the bar, the ballgame was muted, and other screens were dark. Even the trophy bucks were strung with colored bulbs.

"Impressive! It's not even Christmas or March Madness," Will said.

Lights dimmed and Ron, Rosco's current owner, stepped up to the mic, which squealed until his son made adjustments.

A few patrons whistled. Then Ron welcomed everyone, glancing at his prepared notes, saying how honored they were to have authors O.T. Bookman and Lydia Beauvais Galesberg right here at Rosco's. Both waved and smiled. Ron also thanked her and Will from Blackbird for arranging the evening. Will stood, gesturing toward Ron and giving a thumbs-up.

After applause Ron went on, "I've got a clipboard here for sign-ups. Don't be shy, people, there's two slots left. We're going to have a musical number to start us off. Please welcome our own Kelley Rae."

Charlotte cheered along with the crowd. Kelley Rae's twangy country rock had earned her a spot among the final contestants for a national talent search. After her encore came a spoken word call-and-response piece by high school students, followed by a rap number. Among the Rosco's crowd, the rhymes and beats—and somewhat off-putting language—increased the signals for refills. The crowd was warmed up for more, and Will refilled their glasses. Millicent, urged forward by Sarah, read her piece about visiting the Eiffel Tower. The lodge crew and a few others applauded. Charlotte made a reminder on her phone to compliment her later.

Then the time came for one of the major guests, who was introduced, as Charlotte had suggested, by her friend Kate. Wearing a black leotard and peasant skirt, Lydia read for about eight minutes. Though memoir was not in the local taste, her dramatic reading drew polite enthusiasm. Charlotte was relieved to see she looked unperturbed and sat down next to Kate and the library book club.

"What's next?" Will looked around the room. "I hoped we'd get everyone home by ten thirty." She agreed, a huge fatigue settling over her in the warm room, but obviously more readers were ahead.

Ron reminded everyone that the kitchen was still open and looked at his clipboard. "Next up, our own Alice Adamsley from Blackbird Lodge with ah, I guess a poem, called 'What I Thought about before the Aaah . . . Apocalypse.'"

Charlotte felt Will lean closer to be heard over the whistles from Alice's friends. "Did you know about this?"

"She never said a word about a poem on the way here. Maybe something from a college class?" Charlotte felt her heartbeat ratchet up at this public performance, then she upbraided herself and took Will's hand. This was their daughter and they would be proud of whatever she offered.

Ron turned on some mood lights, apparently taking a cue from the title. Alice stepped to center stage and a boy off to the side began a percussive background.

Though Charlotte was pretty sure the crowd couldn't say exactly what the poem was about, its lines spoke to Rosco's people. Heads nodded, fingers caught the percussion line, eyes at the bar strayed from a home run as people anticipated each stanza. A collective sigh came at the last line before finger snapping, table pounding, and applause. Charlotte clapped wildly and tried to restrain Will before he shoved through the chairs to give Alice a papa bear hug. Making a circle, her friends bounced around as she did a victory dance with the musician. Ron signaled refilled pitchers on the house.

So, how about that, Otis? Charlotte kept her victory dance internal. She leaned over as if to pick up her purse in order to take just a glance his way and saw he was already coming toward her.

She opened one hand flat. *Stop.*

He gestured toward Alice. Even across the room his one-word question was clear. "Mine?"

Only your DNA might produce this talented young person? The timing of his interest in her family could not have been more ironic or characteristic. She held his eye a few seconds but couldn't deny the truth. She nodded slightly and turned away, her hands shaking as she waited for Will to return.

Ron took the stage again. "Wow! Now that's a girl we're going to hear more from in years to come." More applause followed. Charlotte stayed seated trying for a blank expression, glad that Will was lingering across the room.

Then Kate received the mic for an introduction of O.T. She said they should be honored that he would read from his upcoming book, giving everyone at Rosco's a sneak preview. O.T. pulled a stool into the spotlight. Charlotte saw Lydia send him a head nod that he ignored.

He had chosen well for the audience, a passage on a man returning to his roots. But something was a little off, Charlotte thought, as if his mind were elsewhere. However, the charisma he radiated without effort, the good humor and wit, touched even the men in the corner betting on the game.

After his reading, as Charlotte watched O.T. get mobbed by the young people, Alice included, she felt the table jar so sharply the pitcher sloshed. Instead of sitting down again, Will yanked his jacket from his chair and left. The set of his shoulders told her he knew.

When she found him in the parking lot, he was flicking between photos of O.T. and Alice at open mic.

"You must think I'm an idiot." He showed her two shots where the resemblance was obvious. "Why did you let this happen?" His voice had a threatening edge she rarely heard.

"Will, we couldn't turn down a group like this. Think of the income we got." She tried to sound reasonable not defensive.

"Is everything about money for you? Besides, I thought you said after the Douglass week we would be okay."

"But they didn't pay full fare, really. And you got better cuts of meat. And—"

"This is all beside the point." He began a quick walk toward the van, throwing out, "You weren't even going to tell me."

She followed along feeling like a dog looking for approval. "Wait . . . not what you think . . ." He didn't stop to listen.

Finally, she caught up. "I didn't even know he was coming until about two weeks beforehand. You would have cancelled the workshop if you knew, so I didn't tell you."

"And you wanted to reconnect!"

"No, not exactly." She needed him to hear her out. Just an apology wouldn't placate his hurt or hers.

"Well, what then?"

"He didn't even remember me, Will, until Thursday." Her voice broke. "I feel ashamed for caring, but I'm upset that—"

"You think you've aged a lot or something?" A spark of amusement cut through his anger.

"Okay, that, and to tell the truth, I helped him a lot with that famous book. But he didn't even remember me or acknowledge my help."

"Whatever. But you owed it to me not to hide this all week."

His disappointment in her was so painful she didn't know whether to reach for him.

"Will, I should have trusted you with his identity. I'm so sorry. Of course, I want that relationship to be over." She explained how she had turned down his advances. "Except there's Alice to think of."

"You think I don't think of her? She is my daughter, always has been. Her welfare is the most important thing in the world to me." Charlotte couldn't overlook his pronoun choices.

He was still frigid when he added, "You didn't tell Alice did you? Behind my back?"

"No, of course not. But right after Alice's poem, he guessed."

Will didn't say a word as she explained how she had caught O.T.'s question from across the room. "I couldn't be dishonest, Will. A lie could hurt Alice in the future. This had to happen sometime—meeting each other." Charlotte sank on a picnic table bench and Will followed.

"Not this way."

She saw how worn out Will looked, his familiar hands trembling.

They talked more about Alice, trying to work through their anxiety about how and when to tell her, wondering if O.T. would make his own announcement. Finally, Will let her lean into him.

"Alice isn't going to think less of you. More, actually. O.T. is kind of a dud in the father department, according to Lydia."

"But famous."

"Alice will think this connection is cool but not significant in her family tree in the long run."

"Char!" he jerked upright nearly upsetting her off the bench. "Does this mean we have to let her have Thanksgiving with him?"

"I hope not!" She pushed away a wealth of other what-ifs related to shared children.

They sat for a few minutes more watching patrons come out for a smoke. Will said they should go back inside, but Charlotte felt she should not be the only one held accountable for nondisclosure.

"Will, wait. Speaking of the past, what about Tabby Douglass's garnet?" She wanted her turn to raise incriminating evidence. "And Auld Lang Syne in the guest book?"

"You noticed." Will made a trip around the table and sat down again heavily. "Goes back to when we were teens and she'd come every year. We hung out at the dock and so on, just like Alice with guests. Except, well, I'm sure Alice doesn't, uh, you know, like Tabby and me."

"When we were eighteen, her old man took me aside, clapped me on the shoulder—still does that—and said now that she was going to Radcliffe in the fall, it was time for me to just look after the boats and help my parents. I got the message. I was a local yokel. She didn't come up with the rest of the family for years after that."

"Go on." *So where was this going?* Charlotte supposed she wanted to know.

"About ten years ago she came back with a husband for Douglass week."

"Strikes me he's a playboy," Charlotte said and was about to add how he got overly familiar after drinks, but Will went on talking as if watching a movie in his head.

"It was weird seeing her after all that time. I knew she was coming and—" His narrative tapered off.

"And?" The parallel to her own situation was bizarre. *What was coming next? Passion in a cabin?*

"Nothing, other than conversation, except this year." Will seemed to have trouble going on. "She told me something from the past."

"Which is?" Charlotte couldn't help herself from prompting Will to keep the story going.

"Apparently that last summer here before college, she got pregnant."

"Oh!"

Will went on to say Tabby got an abortion when her mother found out. Eventually she became a lawyer, not marrying until after her education was complete.

Charlotte saw pain cross his features. *His biological child.* "Would you have married her if you had known?"

"I don't see how that would have worked out. She said at eighteen she couldn't imagine having a baby or getting married. So—it's probably not right, but I got her the garnet. I felt like making some kind of memorial."

Charlotte put her hand in his, a shadow of relief in sight. *This evened the score!* Then she chastised herself for the childish reaction. This was pain he didn't deserve.

"It's a sad story, Will. You did right." Then she added, "You picked out a love knot design though."

"What? Just a crisscross of wire?" His cluelessness seemed genuine. It wasn't the sort of thing a man like Will would take in even if explained in the shop.

They stayed at the table for a while but were too worn out to make a decision about telling Alice. The writer in Charlotte wanted to record these aftermaths somewhere—occurrences so loaded with irony. She had come north looking for other people's stories nineteen years ago. One of their own making had been there all along.

———— • ————

24

An Escape

O.T. saw Charlotte and Will walk out of Rosco's through a side entrance. Considering what could transpire when he next encountered them—a confrontation, fistfight, or demand for money—O.T. decided to hurry out alone. Lydia could ride back in the van, but just as his engine fired, she wrenched open the passenger door.

"I thought I already knew about all the stupid things you did while we were married." She leaned over the console to get closer. "But I see I was wrong."

"What?" *Would she list all his faults again?*

"Do you realize how old that talented girl Alice is?"

"Sixteen?"

"You know she's nineteen."

Lydia held her phone close to his face scrolling by images of Will, then Alice, then him, back and forth, and finally Charlotte, all taken at Rosco's.

"See any similarities?"

He tried to say, "I didn't know," but she had already slammed the door, yelling, "Good luck with explaining this one. You always were a chump."

Where to go? This was the only roadhouse he'd seen, so getting drunk was out of the question. Heading back to Boston in the dark was an option, but he might lose his fee and would miss out on Zenobia. Around the first bend in the road a brown sign directed tourists to an old fire tower trail.

He pulled in. A walk to clear his mind, that's what he needed. The chilly air dried the grotesque dark circles that had formed on his blue shirt. Ordinarily, he wasn't the flop sweat type. *So much for this week being relaxing.*

He staggered along the root-infested trail where the tower loomed at the end. Using his lighter he read a sign cautioning him not to go up the tower stairs, but the barrier gate was ripped off. Obviously other people went up with no problem. He vaulted up a zigzag of stairs to the first platform, which was high but not treetop level, the spruces being nightmarish in height. The steps to the next level were very narrow grates requiring him to tiptoe up. The moon had come out and the view from the platform was something! Trees surrounded him, a battalion so close together their tips formed a wall, and a milky surface lay to his left, maybe a pond. The awesomeness, he never thought he would use that word, did make him feel small, like maybe his problems weren't so important. *But a fourth kid?* This surprise was too much.

He replayed that afternoon with Charlotte and all the years in between. *Why didn't she tell me?* Possible reasons were many. He was married then and she had been his student at one point. Possibly she didn't really like him that much, and she just wanted help with her novel and got pregnant by mistake. *How mortifying!* Earlier that afternoon she had been affable and even tempted for a little outdoor sex, yet she had said nothing about a child.

Maybe she didn't want me to know.

He walked the platform from edge to edge indulging in pleasure over Alice. *What a bright and articulate daughter and beautiful, so like Carly back in the day. How selfish of Charlotte to keep her from me!*

"It's not right," he said aloud.

He considered the possibility that her husband might not know. He looked like a guy who kept his own counsel. O.T. played out other scenarios. Did Charlotte and Alice need rescue from this cold wilderness? He had seen no evidence of this all week. Should he just step aside, leaving his knowledge a secret? Silence would be heroic, tragically heroic—not pressing his paternity, not disturbing their happiness. But then the girl might not learn about the good fortune of her genetic heritage.

He looked up the next zigzag of steps in shadow. Answers might lie above. His foot on the stair, he heard over the sighing of trees a familiar slapping sound.

"Are you up there?"

Cinny's flip-flops carried her up the steps, her head appearing from the dark first, then the rest of her. She sat down panting. "I yelled to you, but you didn't hear so I followed the car."

"On foot?"

"I just wanted to talk." She had her phone in her hand. Perhaps she, too, had incriminating photos she was about to show him.

She pressed an image of the schedule near his face. "The editor will be here tomorrow, so we should figure out writers to recommend."

Oh, God. His relief and fatigue were overwhelming. "Not tonight, not now."

"And there's something else." She let out a long yogic breath. He steeled himself, but at least she couldn't claim pregnancy. "O.T., we haven't talked about my novel revision. Remember, you promised." She touched his arm and leaned in.

Another woman! How often he had heard about promises he had made. *Except from Charlotte.* The realization hit him hard.

"Well, how about tomorrow morning? After breakfast." He might even be gone by then, no telling. He stepped out of her reach.

She sighed again, then turned her tone to optimistic. "I'll knock to make sure you're up. Wow, this is some view up here." She slapped up the first three steps of the stairs leading to the third level and gestured for him to follow.

"No, I'm going back to the lodge." *A quick escape, not a quickie.* He looked down to his car.

With the grates invisible on the way down, locating each step meant feeling around gingerly. He patted his pockets to find his phone for a flashlight. The phone was in his jacket in the car.

"You better not go any further up." He hollered this from the first-level platform, tipping his head back to look for her above. The gesture threw off his balance, and he made an Olympic-worthy cartwheel before landing on the ground.

Or, reconstructing the event, he assumed he landed. The last thing he remembered was the clatter of Cinny in her flip-flops above. Her quick thinking of flagging a car, calling 911 once they found cell service, and riding in the ambulance, she described in dramatic detail later for him and everyone else.

———— • ————

24

— SATURDAY —

Armchair Quarterbacking

AFTER THE COMMOTION FROM THE SIRENS and road flares, and the deputies cooling off at the bar after their shift, news of the professor's fall had reached everyone at Rosco's. All the stress and staying late at the hospital made Saturday breakfast a trial for Will. He moved by automatic motions, cooking and fielding questions about communications they had received. He was as concerned as everyone else, but for different reasons and possibly with different hopes of the outcome. Charlotte, also completely drained, was in her office on the phone again, calling whom he wasn't sure. Lydia went back to the hospital. Alice, as astonished by the accident as the writers, was taking the sensible recourse of sleeping in. Will was gratified about that.

In the dining room, Cinny was reliving the night's details for the group, trying to explain their climb up the tower. He wondered if she would offer any other revelations about O.T.

"Do we know why he was up the fire tower?" Bea's question got to the heart of the matter. Will lingered by the buffet rechecking the cream and milk pitchers. All eyes were on Cinny.

"He's, ah, spontaneous sometimes. Maybe he wanted quiet after the readings?"

Hiding from me, more likely, Will thought and felt a twinge of satisfaction again. Charlotte said at the hospital that this motive for the climb seemed unlikely, but he had countered, "You don't know men as well as you think!"

"I hope he's not depressed!" Sarah's concern sounded genuine.

"Oh, no! I don't think so."

Westley contradicted Cinny's denial. "Writers have a dark side, you know. Hemingway, Virginia Woolf, Sylvia Plath."

"Dr. Bookman's psyche seems very solid to me," Ruth said.

Will found Westley's speculation disturbing. The tower presented only two options—up and down. Yes, death would take the extra dad out of the picture, but a suicide could have a devastating effect on Alice.

"You two were together?" Millicent emphasized the final word, not bothering to hide her thoughts on Cinny's miraculous presence.

"Not actually. I found him up there." She described again her run behind his car.

"How fortunate for us you are such a sprinter." Westley went on, speculating with, "Maybe he was drunk."

"No, no, he tripped at the edge, but I couldn't catch hold of him." Will found her demonstration convincing. Wiping away tears, she added, "It was terrible."

Ruth spoke up cutting off the spurious suggestions. "I can only imagine. So lucky you were there." She put her arm around Cinny, who looked genuinely distressed as the comments continued.

"Where's Lydia? She must be distraught, you know, even though they . . ." No one finished the sentence.

"And today the editor is coming. What about that?" Millicent asked for everyone. Will could see the writers had concerns even without knowing of his own.

Discussion continued about the weirdness of accidents, the quality of the local medical group, and the chances for quick recovery. Obviously, they hoped the accident wouldn't derail the highlight of the week, the visitor from New York City. Cinny promised she and Lydia would carry on. No worries.

Will piled up the dishes, deciding no more clarity had emerged about the accident, or the father-daughter connection.

A bare spot on the wall brought him to a halt as he headed toward Charlotte's office. *What the hell?* Last night's revelations changed a lot of things, but not the gallery of Whitehead and Adamsley pictures. Maybe the heavy frame had fallen down and Charlotte failed to mention it. *Like a lot of other things this week.* He was sure the picture had been there recently, the black-and-white photo of Cleveland Whitehead at middle age sitting in a throne-like chair, a gun was across his lap, a Bible in his right hand. A peculiar composition, in Will's opinion, dated 1929 on the gold frame.

The missing portrait was something to investigate later. Right now, he'd like to be alone outdoors hiking up a mountain trail where a man could think clearly, get a perspective. *Maybe Bookman had the same inclination when he went up the fire tower.* But no solitary hour was available because he had to carry on here. Maybe Charlotte had news. Maybe it was time to tell Alice.

———— • ————

26

Visiting Hours, Family Only

The feeling was like one of the half-asleep states O.T. had where he couldn't open his eyes—sleep paralysis. Though he had been told the event was harmless, the feeling had terrified him in the past. Nonetheless, right now he felt peaceful. Perhaps this was what death was like. Through closed lids he sensed a bright light. All the testimonies about floating above one's body with no desire to return and the tunnel of white light seemed right. All the elements were in place. He drifted, waiting for what was next.

Words floated to him.

"I still don't understand. Why was he up a ladder with you? Aren't you his student helper?" Luella said. Two sobs and a long sniff followed.

"Is Dad drinking again?" His oldest son was speaking.

"No, of course not, but tell me how this—" Luella began but was cut short by Lydia.

"Your father was always doing crazy things with his precious grad students."

"Oh, lay off, Mom. That was a long time ago." Son Number 2 went on, "This isn't the time for a trip down memory lane."

"It wasn't a ladder." Cinny jumped in. "He went up an old fire tower for the view, I guess."

"The view at night." Luella spoke with sarcasm, then sobbed again. O.T. felt his eyelids twitch and his pupils roll back and forth.

Cinny continued, "Maybe doing the reading was stressful and he decided to climb the tower to cool off. Then—I don't know how—on the platform his foot slipped. Then he did a cartwheel off the edge. It was so awful." Her voice was muffled as she wept into a tissue or something. O.T. shuddered.

Luella addressed Cinny. "You promised to look after him. That was your only job. I told him a quiet summer at home would help with his book, after a little texting incident that nearly got him fired."

Would she ever forget this?

"I just should have insisted on no traveling. Now look at him."

No doubt Lydia was finding this naivete hilarious. O.T. was impressed by her restraint in front of the boys, who seemed more sensible in the face of crisis than the rest of them.

Son Number 1: "Dad can you hear us?" He leaned in and spoke loudly.

Son Number 2: "We're here for you, Dad. Mom and Luella and, what's your name again?"

"Cinny, short for Cynthia."

A nurse intervened over the beeping monitors. "Just let me turn this morphine drip down. He should be able to respond in a few minutes. We knocked him out last night for evaluation."

A wave of pain convinced O.T. that he wasn't dead, nor would he be soon. He kept his eyes closed. *What next?*

"Now about his royalties. We should talk about that while he's still out." Lydia's tone was all business.

"Christ. Mom, he's not dead," came from Son Number 1.

"No, but this is a good time for clarity. I want you boys to know how things stand. The divorce decree says royalties from his books go to his children in the event of his passing." Lydia sounded as if she had moved away from the bedside.

"Now wait a minute here." Luella was shrill and moved toward him. "You forget he has a daughter too."

"Royalties from books written before any second marriage go to his children from our marriage," Lydia said.

"That lets out this last manuscript." Luella had a triumphant note in her voice. "And it's almost completed."

Lydia snorted. "The famous seminal work? Don't bank your girl's tuition on that one. He's been working on that for years."

"It is almost finished." Cinny's remark held a note of firm optimism. *Nice of her to defend me.*

"In fact," Luella intoned her insider information, "he told me he's been very productive this week. I'm sure the book will be snapped up, probably auctioned."

Finally, she let their toddler come to the bed. O.T. could catch her baby scent.

"You are married, aren't you?" Lydia said.

"We've been together for five years and—"

"So, you're not married?" Lydia pounced on this delicious morsel.

"Certainly in every sense of the word. Now if you'll all just leave us alone, I'd like quiet time here with Oatie and our daughter before I go back to the lodge to clear out his things."

"Wait a minute, you two!" Cinny's yell brought him into full consciousness. He raised his lids to a slit. "The way you're bickering is disrespectful. He's going to make it. He has to. He's my thesis advisor. And besides that, my manuscript and his are in his room, so if anyone clears things out, I should be the one."

O.T. saw movement near the window. Carly-Charlotte stood there with—*Yes, Alice!*

He could avoid engagement no longer. For one thing, he needed more of that morphine drip soon. *Or some of them might need it.* Not moving his head, he opened his eyes fully and looked around as if confused. But he wasn't really. He just wanted to see them—these women who were each mad at him for different reasons—he loved them all!

Each had given him something, well, two sons and two daughters, apparently, but more than that, they had made him feel important and he had made them feel loved, he knew he had. Maybe imperfectly. *I am kind of a rogue. Or no, a tragic hero! My flaw, loving too much.* He had brought out something good in each one.

They converged on his bed, and he smiled hearing the monitor bleep along confirming he really was alive. He hoped his hair looked good. A strident voice jarred his silent soliloquy.

"I'm sorry but just family here. The rest of you have to leave." An imposing-sounding woman spoke from the door and came in. When no one moved, she added, "You want him to recover, don't you?"

O.T. waited for their response.

"Folks! The only people who can stay are partners, blood relations, and parents of blood relations." She looked from Lydia, to Luella, to Cinny, and to Charlotte and Alice. Only Cinny flounced out.

More lucidity and pain were hitting him by the second as he saw Alice take her mother's hand and pull her to the door. *Someone needed to say something.*

"Not you! Don't leave!" He found he had shouted and saw the line on the monitor leap. "Alice! You're mine too. Last night . . . Carly, you've always been in my—"

He could say nothing more. Someone had dialed up the morphine drip.

"Excuse me. Is that the author O.T. Bookman?"

In his flock of women she was unheard. "I'm from Daly Books in New York. Netta Simpson, assistant to the editors." She held out her small hand, but no one took it.

———•———

27

A Mother-Daughter Talk

Alice felt her mother nudge her out past the others standing by the now silent bed. *What is wrong with these people?* Alice amended her designation. *My people.*

When her mother went to start the van, Alice put her finger over the ignition. "So, Mom . . . Mom?" They weren't going to just drive off without her learning about this father. Maybe she was in shock, but it felt more like a high, the good kind. She stared at her mom.

"You weren't going to tell me?"

"This wasn't the way your dad and I wanted to tell you, Allie. But I thought you should come to the hospital in case—"

"Dr. Bookman passed away?" The phrase sounded less final than died and more poetic. *He might like that.* Her mother had loved this guy, apparently, back in the day.

"What a shock for you, honey." Alice ducked the hug she saw coming as her mom continued apologizing. "I'm so sorry. I never thought he would say anything outright to you. And in front of everyone."

Her mom was shaking her head. "But that's him all over. Everything is drama. You'd think I'd know after all the times we—"

Alice moved her hand away from the ignition. Maybe she didn't want to know everything right now.

"Never mind that part, Mom. I knew something was up all week. You didn't get upset about my hair and you didn't argue about Roy staying over. And mostly—"

"What?"

"You've been wearing a lot of weird old clothes."

"I don't think so!"

"The tie-dye dress, really? But I get it now. And then he didn't recognize you, did he?" *That would really suck.*

"Not until Thursday."

Her mom always looked the same, sensible outdoor-style clothes like everybody's mom, with her hair usually pulled back, makeup sometimes. She had never considered whether her mom had been very different or looked very different before. *Like a Carly?*

"Dr. Bookman was a jerk not to recognize you." Alice offered the hug this time and noticed her mom's hair had been shaped, even highlighted, but the time had passed to say something nice about it.

Her mom didn't say more, just chose a shortcut, turning onto a one-lane road that ended near the lodge. On the sand-filled tracks, the van slewed, as did Alice's thoughts.

What if Mom and Dr. Bookman got together again?

She might move to Boston with them, her dad left behind for the long winter in the lodge alone. Would he know the attic light comes on only by pounding on the switch plate? *I could write that down.* And putting away the boats. They always had the big fall party for that. He would build a fire on the beach and serve his special mac and cheese, and they would make pumpkin ice cream from the old crank freezer. Her mom would sit out with him after everyone left, "being romantic" they said and laughed.

No, we will not be moving to Boston. Her mom and dad were rock solid. *Weren't they?*

"Having a second father may be interesting for you." As usual her mom was trying to find a bright side. "He's rather well known."

"It'll be no big deal. Almost everyone I know has a step-family or half-sibs. How about the people by the store who all live in the same house? And people at college have two moms. My roommate has a sperm donor for a dad." Alice knew she was rattling along over unimportant proof until she got to a troubling idea.

"Is Dad having a heart attack over this?"

"Not yet."

Good. Her mom was smiling. One of them asked this about once a month, her dad being often unreadable when drama arose.

"Maybe he wants to punch Dr. Bookman!" This would be interesting—like a movie or book but upsetting.

"Quite possibly."

Something even more awful occurred to Alice. "Is this all my fault?"

"Is what your fault?"

"That Dad found out. If I hadn't read last night, Dr. Bookman wouldn't have noticed me. You could have kept your, your secret." She could feel tears coming.

"No, it wasn't mine to keep forever. Maybe this way was good. I was looking for the right time to tell you both, but that can mean never finding a time at all."

With so much to process, Alice got out of the van and went around to the back of the lodge to avoid more parental encounters.

——— • ———

28

Tit for Tat

He looks good even out cold. Netta settled on her opinion as she was ushered away by the nurse. What with the firm jawline with distinct shadow, the cared-for careless hair, he looked as if he came right off a cruise ad. He would be touching champagne flutes with a trophy wife in front of an impossibly blue ocean. The editorial intimacy she had pictured, something he had given freely at other times apparently, now seemed unlikely this weekend.

The bio details she had dug up matched these people, except for the surprise daughter. *What a story!* Fact being stranger than fiction, etc., etc. She probably should have waited at the lodge, as Mr. Adamsley advised, but Zenobia would expect a complete report about the accident. She wouldn't disappoint on this front at least.

A young woman in rumpled sweats addressed her sharply after they were hustled out as nonfamily. "Where is Zenobia Daly? Is she coming later?"

"No. I'm representing Daly House. And you are . . . ?"

"I'm the workshop coordinator and O.T.'s graduate assistant, Cynthia. Cinny for short." She didn't offer her hand. "So, it's just you from Daly?" Netta noted the emphasized pronoun even before Cinny added, "We were expecting the editor-in-chief. The writers and O.T. are going to be disappointed."

"Frankly, it doesn't look as if Dr. Bookman is going to have much to say at all." Netta straightened her Daly House book bag on her shoulder. Unlike this grad assistant, she had a job in New York publishing and a completed MFA. Then, Cinny's next remark made her sympathetic.

"People shouldn't think it was my fault he fell. No one told him to go up that fire tower." She seemed to be addressing an inquest near the emergency entrance where a police car was parked.

"It's a free country" was all Netta could think of for reassurance. As the Daly rep she needed to lay the groundwork for success with this assistant. She offered Cinny a ride to the lodge, asked about the workshop activities, and complimented her on the variety.

"I'll be managing the schedule of writers you'll meet with tonight and tomorrow," Cinny said, adding as if publishing was a casual interest of hers, "How many manuscripts have you sold?"

Netta gripped the steering wheel. The question at the heart of her career success felt aggressive, but honesty might build their relationship, she reminded herself.

"None, quite yet." She went on to describe her responsibilities with the slush pile and the editors' meetings, casting a golden glow on the poisonous competition.

"You're looking for the hidden gem, right?"

"Yeah, something outstanding and that will sell."

The conversation lapsed into current reading favorites, their MFA experiences, and the job market. Where the road skirted the edge of a steep bank, Netta thought of how a driving mishap could result in the ICU. She refocused on the present. "You're going to show me some efforts from the senior citizens tonight?"

"Yes, the writers."

Was Cinny being patronizing? Netta glanced from the rolling blacktop to conclude the enthusiasm seemed genuine.

"Now that we've worked them hard all week, several show promise, as your people at Daly will see."

Zenobia could care less. Netta smiled stiffly toward her passenger. To Zenobia, the important result was positive PR with charming photos for Daly House advertising. She parroted her boss, "I'm excited to see the results and Daly House may—"

"Actually," Cinny's demeanor changed to hopeful author, "I'm in the final revision of the first book of my YA series."

Here comes the elevator talk. Netta adopted her polite interest veneer bracing for a plot synopsis.

"Having a professional editor like you take a look at, oh, you know, the first chapter, would mean so much to me."

Netta began a reappraisal of the weekend's potential, how circumstances could be manipulated to bring back something marketable. After all, Cinny was in an MFA presumably studying under, or advised by, Bookman. That needed to be defined.

"Yes, I could make time for that. Are you close with Dr. Bookman?" She could see an exchange of favors, manuscript help for Cinny smoothing the way for her spending time with Bookman. They would talk about his impending manuscript, her editorial skill a beacon leading him to Daly House, then a sympathetic scene where his appreciation was obvious.

"Close? You mean—" Cinny's gesture clarified.

Netta laughed then jerked the tires from the edge of the road where boulders blacked out her writer-and-his-editor scene. "I meant have you read his latest manuscript?"

"Oh, yes. I have assisted in editing, and so forth." Netta wanted to ask about the manuscript's potential but that could wait.

"What's it like to work with someone so talented and famous?"

"Well, he's very needy in some ways." Again, Cinny didn't elaborate.

Netta had heard the senior editors coddle, wheedle, and even threaten writers on the phone. "Needy" was where she could fit in. "What happened to him here was just terrible, really bad luck. I hope he makes it, I mean, back to the workshop."

"I'll make sure to mention your interest in his manuscript, and I'll give you mine, as soon as we get back."

✍

In the front hall at Blackbird Lodge, Charlotte and Lydia were conversing as if nothing awkward lay between them when Netta arrived with Cinny in tow. Lydia apologized to Netta for ignoring her at the hospital.

"Let's find your room. This must be so upsetting after driving all this way. But not to worry, we'll make the best of it."

The four of them went up the stairs.

"Here's your room." Charlotte opened the door to the best room, which she had reserved for Zenobia and was now giving to a young woman hardly older than Alice. The girl looked thrilled and dropped her backpack inside. Charlotte pointed out Lydia's room and Cinny's.

Lydia touched the door across the hall. "This is Dr. Bookman's, but I doubt he'll be back tonight." Charlotte caught an amused glance sent her way as Lydia added, "He should rest in any case."

"Cynthia," Charlotte resumed formality as host, "please let the group know that we packed box lunches for today because of so much, well, so much confusion. Guests may pick up a lunch at one. Dinner will be the usual time. You will hear the bell. Tonight is our barbeque, always a lodge favorite."

Charlotte didn't apologize for the lunch that they threw together from pantry odds and ends, a tuna or chicken salad sandwich, a store-bought cookie, and an apple. To ensure the last day ended on a high note despite the accident, Lydia informed her she had extended the time for the Daly House sessions through Sunday morning. This would be an inconvenience but trivial in light of everything else.

She and Will were navigating around the real issues between them. No matter his feelings, Will would counsel himself to focus on what was best for his Alice. Did she believe no recent physical intimacies had occurred between him and Tabby? *Pretty much.* Last night she refrained from checking old guest book entries for more veiled messages from Tabby.

Fortunately, Lydia had taken over the wife role, speaking with physicians and making arrangements with O.T.'s insurance. After the hospital revelation, Luella announced that with a toddler, she needed a modern resort and drove to Saranac Lake. Lydia's sons were going to a nearby campground but promised they would come back for dinner.

———— • ————

29

What's in a Name?

A GETTING-TO-KNOW-MY-FATHER EXPEDITION was called for, Alice decided. She drove back to the hospital midafternoon while her parents were huddled in her mom's office. They weren't the yelling kind of couple, but they certainly had issues to discuss, and she'd just as soon skip any discord and evade any heartfelt family meetings.

When she got to the second floor of the hospital, she was trembling, a result of the uncertainties she hadn't considered until she stood outside his room. *He might not want to see me now. Or ever.* Child support, fear of her dad, anger at her mom—these could all change the interest Professor O.T. Bookman had shown her yesterday. *Well, whatever.* She could always leave in a hurry.

He was propped up in bed and looking less pathetic in a dark T-shirt, even though he had staples in his forehead like Frankenstein's monster. Somebody had brought him his own clothes. *My mom?*

She knocked on the open door. "May I come in, ah, Dr. Bookman?"

"Of course." So far, he looked pleased to see her. "Honey, come over here so I can see you up close."

"It's Alice, Alice Elizabeth."

"Of course, sorry, I didn't mean to overstep. You're just such a surprise. A welcome one!" He wanted to hug her she could see, but that meant climbing on the bed. She held out her hand instead, and he wrapped both of his around hers. "Your mom never told you who—"

She wasn't here to discuss her mom. "My dad and I always knew he's not biological. I just wanted to say this up front. He's my dad." She felt tears coming, but crying wasn't in her plan.

"I can see what a great guy he is. And the lodge is a wonderful place to grow up."

"I guess." Suddenly North Country did seem wonderful— the lakes and mountains, her friends, and the lodge guests.

A scuffle at the door interrupted her description of mountain winters.

"We brought some chicken, Dad. Oh, sorry, you have company."

Until this morning she had been an only child. These were her half-brothers, older and reasonably good-looking.

"Maybe he shouldn't be eating fried chicken," Alice said feeling superior in her good judgment already. "I'll bring him," she gestured toward the bed, "some of my dad's chicken noodle soup for supper. I'm sure that would be healthier."

They put the chicken wings back in the bag. The older one said, "I'm Nate, for Nathan, and this is Whitney, or Whit."

"Oh, I know. I looked you up online already."

"Now we're in trouble." They both laughed.

"What did the tests show?" The cuter one, who was older, looked at a printout lying on the bed.

"Nothing more than some bruises. I'm good for another fifty years, you'll be disappointed to know."

"Dad!" The sons said in unison, but she couldn't join in before settling on a name for this father.

"So how about if you call him Dad and I call him, ah, . . ." She cast around for what felt right.

"How about Paw-paw?"

"Or Pops . . . or there's always Father."

The brothers riffed until interrupted.

"No, no! Pops sounds like an old radio show. Father makes me sound ancient, like Jacob with the twelve sons."

"Is this your way of saying there are more sons somewhere, Dad?" Whit said, both kidding and not kidding, it seemed to her. His father grimaced.

That is my brother Whit. Alice tried out the phrase silently.

"I tried out 'DNA Dad,' but my mom freaked." She couldn't resist adding to their list.

"No doubt. I shall remain Captain Nemo for the time being." This father seemed wittier than her other one.

Nate sent her a grin. "You could call him Otis, or O.T. That's very modern."

"Oh, no! The most modern is to use the plural pronoun 'they.' Like, 'I am bringing they chicken soup.'"

"In case I'm gender fluid after this head bump?" The not-Dad went on in a kind way, "Let it rest, Alice. You'll find the right words for us soon." He lowered his bed, adding, "I'm bushed, you guys. Take the chicken and find a picnic table somewhere."

"Yes, our pater needs to rest." Nate collected the bag and sodas.

Alice had pulled her hand from O.T. when the brothers arrived but offered it again before they went out. He really did look like the photo on the back of his famous book. *Maybe this will all work out.*

On the way downstairs, Whit said, "Probably Daddy-o is out too."

———— • ————

30

Meanwhile, Back at the Lodge

THE PORCH CHAIRS WERE FULL Saturday afternoon as the writers waited for news, either about O.T. or about the editor's reactions to their work. The Adamsleys were out of sight, and Lydia and Cinny were in the library sharing impressions with Netta, who took notes.

Ruth brought her rocker to a halt, took Westley's book from her bag, and leaned toward him. "I snatched this book from Millicent when I saw your name on the cover." She showed the cover around provocatively eliciting an "oh, my" from Sarah.

"Yes, we found it first-rate," Bea said, adding, "with a clever plot. Why, the setting of Akron works like a character itself."

Westley nodded in a grand way.

"I liked it a lot too," Millicent said. "I told Westley, 'Don't be shy over your publishing success.'" She put her hand on his shoulder.

"Well, just my little murder mystery."

Anticipating his reach for the book, Ruth tipped back in the rocker. "Akron was your home?"

"Oh, no, Syracuse." Millicent took over as promoter since Westley was silent.

"Not a hometown, then. You build the sense of place so well." Then Ruth embellished further. "The big lake and so forth." She gestured with arms wide.

When Westley said nothing, she let Bea take over.

"Ruth and I have argued about Detective Cleeg. Now, what do you think he would have done if Camila had double-crossed him?" Bea leaned toward Westley for insider information.

"That's a plot twist for a good reader like you to unravel, don't you think?"

Ruth thought his toothy smile was faked and wasn't surprised when he checked his watch and stood. Millicent laughed and held him back. "Come on, do tell us. Or will that be in the sequel?"

"A sequel. How ambitious!" Sarah clapped and added that she would order his first book online.

Ruth flipped some pages still not surrendering the book. The time had come to play her trump. "You describe someone as a 'blatherskite.' I'm not familiar with that word. It means—?"

"Refers to an occupation," Westley said and again readied to leave.

"Ah, something in Akron steel manufacture, a blathering process perhaps?" Ruth nodded as if now educated.

"Related to metal. I couldn't explain engineering to you now," he said, disappearing into the lodge.

Or ever, Ruth thought, refraining from looking at Bea.

After he left, Sarah said, reading from her phone, "First use 1650, a talkative person, a blatherskite."

Millicent added, "I don't think Akron is on Lake Erie. Well, maybe we could call it artistic license."

"I just threw that in to check his geography. Maybe we should say he didn't write this book at all." Ruth returned it to Millicent. The women were silenced by this suggestion and chairs squeaked as they gazed at their lake.

Will was in the kitchen preparing for the Saturday night extravaganza of barbequed pork, salmon, and steak on skewers with summer vegetables. Yes, a big grill would be better, an outdoor kitchen sort of thing, but his old barrel, if fired up and loaded just right, worked perfectly. He heard someone stamping along the walk outside. Another surprise was more than he could take.

"Adamsley!" The one male guest—creepy, Alice had called him—was coming inside carrying the missing portrait.

"I'd like to talk with you man-to-man. I'm not a person to make a scene."

Men who said this were the type to make a scene, Will figured and moved behind the heavy farmhouse table. "What's on your mind?"

"I'm going to store the portrait of Whitehead in my cabin."

Will considered his options. He went for open-minded. "And why is that?"

"Because it's mine." The man put a fist on the table.

"You want to buy it?"

"I don't need to. Whitehead is my great-great-uncle. I'm the remaining heir."

"Really? I can see you'd like a portrait." Will thought of his mother's rule to please the guests. "We may have another one upstairs you could have. 'Course, I'd like to know evidence of your claim."

"Here's my evidence, you North Country nobody." As Westley reached in his shirt, Will lunged for the knife block. Instead of producing a weapon, the man threw documents on the table.

"You left out one part of the entertaining story you told the other night."

"What do you mean?" The knives were within his reach, not Westley's.

"Whitehead was drunk so your George Adamsley forged the document that deeded the property. No honest judge would uphold the claim to the deed, but then convenient fires in the county courthouse, country lawyers, ignorant judges, complicit cronies. The facts are all here in this document I've researched." Westley pounded the table.

"You'll hear from my lawyer. Better start packing." He flung open the screen door with such force that one hinge came off. "All of your people let this place go all to shit."

He turned back. "Listen, Adamsley, I'll do you a favor. I won't mention this tonight. I wouldn't want to ruin the horse meat barbecue for the ladies."

Fortunately for Westley, the table prevented Will from delivering the punch that had been meant for O.T. until the accident made it undeliverable. His arm had remained bowstring taut, ready for release. Thinking of Alice had kept his inclinations in check. About Charlotte's feelings, he was less concerned. They had some bridges to rebuild.

He went into the hallway where the Adamsley and Whitehead photos hung. The silhouette from the missing portrait boded ill. The faded rectangle looked like a passage into another world, like the mirror in the looking glass book his Alice had him read again and again. Just rehanging Whitehead wouldn't eliminate the other world that had materialized at Rosco's—Bookman and his women and children, a wonderland from which Will could see no exit.

And now this. He stood in front of his great-grandfather's wedding photo and said, "His claim's bogus."

The taxes came every year, and Adamsleys had always paid them. What other proof of ownership did he and Charlotte need? Yet, the worry lingered. In the attic was a strongbox of papers his father said they would go over together some-day, a day that never came. Will had left the box unopened. Demands of the lodge day-to-day and the richness of family life left little curiosity about the contents.

He returned to the kitchen without telling Charlotte the latest news.

☙

After naps in the Bluebird cabin, Bea and Ruth were giddy with anticipation for their coup de grâce.

"There he goes now." Ruth spotted him first.

Bea yanked open their door. "Westley, can you step in to help us? We're in a dither getting ready to meet the editor tomorrow morning."

"Talking to that girlie looks like a waste of time." He hesitated on the walk.

"Maybe favor us with an opinion? Just let us read you our synopsis." Ruth gestured pressing palms together.

"Obviously we would value your suggestions. We're so nervous about showing it to anyone." Bea opened the door even wider, sweeping her hand invitingly. "We can offer a scotch." He came in.

Ruth handed him a drink and showed him to a seat by the window. They pulled up their chairs close so he couldn't budge.

"Here goes! Be ruthless now in your criticism!" Ruth cleared her throat and began.

"Peter Goodfellow, anxious to finish his novel, rents a quiet cottage in the mountains. Little does he know that the surprise ending he seeks is close at hand." Ruth dropped her voice dramatically.

"The character name is trite," Westley said taking a sip of his scotch.

"Oh, good point. I'll change it. Let's see, how about Cathcart?" Bea leaned over to scribble on the page then urged, "Go on, Ruth."

"Every day he writes and some days he tours the countryside."

Westley yawned widely and drained his glass. "No action? You should have action up front."

Ruth made a marginal note and continued. "One night our protagonist—that's Cathcart—is bored and visits a local bar. The companions are engaging, one man in particular, whom he describes as a blatherskite, is also writing a book."

"Ah, that word again," Bea said and offered a refill of scotch.

Westley demurred, checked his watch, and made a move to get up, but Bea's rocking chair was in his way. "Oh, dinner's not for a few minutes yet. Do humor us with more suggestions."

"Goodfellow's, or sorry, Cathcart's new companion suggests an excellent fishing spot that's very private." Ruth paused. "Our hero goes there one day, sure that the fresh air will shake out the plot ending he's been seeking."

Bea took over. "Little does he expect that this is his ending, in fact. He drowns, leaving his manuscript in his cottage. Now the rest of the story is about the lady detectives who—"

"Ridiculously ill developed." Westley tried to shove back Bea's chair, but she settled more squarely.

"But I didn't finish," Ruth flapped the pages. "The lady detectives discover the blatherskite went on to publish the book under his own name, making them surmise this person guessed the manuscript would be in Cathcart's mountain cottage and that Cathcart might not return until late afternoon, if ever."

Bea said, "More scotch? What do you think of the plot, Westley?"

"Improbable and baseless!"

"Not so. Cathcart described you perfectly in his cabin guest book."

As they anticipated, Westley lunged for the guest book on the table.

"That's just a dummy." Bea tapped it with her fingers.

Ruth went on, "Now I agree there are a few holes in the story, probably something a local detective might be interested in helping us with now that we know who Cathcart met at Rosco's." She put the bottle out of reach lest it become a weapon.

"But we're ready to deal," Bea leaned in close to Westley. "Charlotte and Will seem like nice people. It would be a shame to drag them through a flimflam lodge claim challenge. Maybe you're thinking better of that now?"

The women pulled back their chairs allowing him to stand.

"Just put that portrait right back on the wall, and we'll make some changes in our synopsis, leaving out the blatherskite. But if—"

"Huh! You can't prove a thing." Westley set down his glass and twiddled his scarf grandly. "Look at the shape this place is in, a fine camp left to go to ruin. I wouldn't take back this white elephant if they paid me."

"So, we're square?" Ruth said.

"Square."

Bea moved her rocking chair so he could take a step. He muttered something on his way out.

"He just called us old biddies," Bea said.

"No doubt he meant you."

"The word was plural, but we should be flattered. So much classier than bitches."

"Let's drink to that!" Ruth took a swig and passed the bottle to Bea.

———— • ————

34

— SUNDAY —

Ride Sharing

From a physician assistant on Sunday, O.T. learned that he'd been very lucky. He didn't have any significant injury that the tests could reveal at the small hospital, only a cracked collarbone and heavy bruising. He decided to check himself out. Also, he feared overdoing the morphine drip that was so easy to request.

However, he needed a ride to the lodge. Options were limited. Cinny couldn't bring his car because he had the keys. Distraught over learning that he had yet another offspring, Luella had swept Maddie back to Boston that morning. His sons were camping. Lydia had her Mustang, but he didn't need another scolding. Apparently, Zenobia hadn't come at all—*so like her to avoid leaving the city*—though he had thought she would show up for him. The lodge people should have the responsibility to come get him, a guest. Phone in hand, he reconsidered. *Suppose Carly's husband showed up?*

Instead, he called a ride-sharing app. A driver was ready for him within minutes, introducing herself and apologizing because she couldn't help him to the car on account of her game leg.

"Not to worry, I'm tough. I just need some rest." He edged into the back seat next to a pile of recycling.

"Just give that a shove. Adamsleys will treat you good. No doubt of that." She swung the Buick onto the highway.

"You know them?" He leaned forward as close as the seat belt allowed.

"Will's a local boy, goes way back with me." She drove glancing often at the rearview mirror.

"His wife?"

"Oh, Charlotte, she's from somewhere else." She waved her hand dismissively. "Came here to work at Lake Placid. Met Will."

"When was that?"

"Let's see that would be about when Will's folks died. About nineteen years ago but seems like yesterday. His mother and I were close." She held up two fingers twined together.

"They have just one child?"

"Ayup, Alice. Don't know what happened there. Women's troubles probably."

"Ah."

"'Course running that lodge would wear anyone down. And hardly any income in the winter. Too far from the ski places."

He hadn't ridden in a back seat this large in twenty years. He wished the lodge was farther. Maybe there was more to learn about the Adamsleys. "Their daughter read quite a piece at Rosco's Friday night."

"So I heard. Made her folks proud. 'Course, all that talent comes right from her mother."

"You think?"

"Oh, sure. People say Charlotte's standoffish. She's a deep thinker is all. Us gals will be rattling along about whatever, and she's quiet 'til she comes out with something said just perfect." She laughed and shook her head. "I wonder how Will puts a word in at home, her and Alice being so smart."

"He's a good-natured guy, is he?"

"That's not the word I'd use, but he's local, you know. Everyone respects him and he returns the favor."

At the lodge, O.T. edged out of the Buick and gave a big tip. His driver's assessment of Will helped him decide that checking in with Cinny, Lydia, or any Adamsleys could wait. He went slowly to the dock.

☞

The writers had several hours free before their final meeting. Netta knew she needed to make the most of the day. Soon she was to drive back to New York, and she hadn't accomplished anything yet. She had not had any intimacy, literary or otherwise, with O.T., had not chosen a manuscript among the writers, and instead had spent time with Cinny. In a final bit of procrastination to keep from choosing a manuscript, she went down to the dock and was startled when O.T. came out of the boathouse in a canoe.

"Wow! You're back!" She felt embarrassed for such a juvenile remark.

"I feel much better this morning, but you look glum. Have we met?"

"I'm Netta Simpson, from Daly House." She realized a handshake was impossible and waved instead.

"Nice to meet you. I heard Zenobia bailed. Get in, we'll go for a paddle."

He steadied the canoe as she climbed in the front, thinking this might be irresponsible. *Suppose he blacks out and tips us over?*

"Netta. What a lovely name. Now, what's the trouble?"

"I'm hiding from the writers. They're all just so nice." She knew how to paddle and began a strong stroke to preserve his energies.

"How can you ever be an editor if you can't reject anyone?" He matched his strokes to hers and went on. "'Not what we're looking for currently.' 'Not within our genre needs.'" He quoted phrases she sent out by the dozen every week.

"'We must decline the opportunity to represent you,'" Netta added. "That's called a positive tone rejection. I think it sounds like the royal family." Amusing him was easy, as she could see was happening. *Maybe he will offer his manuscript.*

"Those letters are all drivel." He guided the canoe toward the middle of the lake despite her angling her paddle to keep them around the shore. "How do you like being in publishing? Or working for Zenobia? We go way back."

Even with the staples in his forehead, he was as appealing as his retouched jacket photo. She decided to try honesty. "I'm not getting anywhere at Daly House because I haven't found a terrific manuscript that will sell. I'll probably never find one if they only give me the slush pile. Besides, Zenobia says I have no sense of what's marketable." She wished she could withdraw her last remark, not wanting to sound like a whiner.

O.T. guided them to a little rocky island. Though he was the one convalescing, he took her hand to help her out on a twig-strewn bank where they sat down. *Now what?*

☙

"Maybe I can help you," O.T. said. These professionals were alarmingly young. He hoped he looked at her in a way she would call amused, not suggestive. "You're overlooking what's right in front of you."

"You mean, your manuscript? I would be, be so—" Her professional cool melted sweetly as she met his gaze fully.

"Mine?" He lay back on the pebbly sand to escape her enthusiasm. He toyed with the idea, a new editor unjaded and enthusiastic by his side. From this angle he could see the lodge across the lake reminding him to stick with the idea that came to him last night.

"No, Charlotte Adamsley. She has a manuscript." Yes, at Ann Arbor he had been jealous of her talent, even thinking her perceptive coming-of-age story would keep while he monopolized her energies for his manuscript.

"The innkeeper? Have you read it?"

"Not recently, but I'm sure the book will be thoughtful and engaging, something that sells." He could see people come out onto the lodge porch. It appeared to be Alice and her mother with others.

"I don't know. She seems kind of, well, stuck here."

"Reclusive? Maybe."

"I'm not sure what my boss would say if I asked the innkeeper, not a workshop person, to come to New York." The assistant to the assistant editor's face flushed at the potential for wrath if she went rogue.

"Trust me," O.T. said. He touched her cheek. "Charlotte has your hidden gem. And don't be afraid of Zenobia. Tell her I remember all the good times at the Algonquin. She'll laugh."

Zenobia had been a beginner at his first publisher. Terrified by the noted editor assigned to him, he spent time with Zenobia, who reassured him that they saw a best seller in his debut novel. Evenings they walked Manhattan, often standing outside the Algonquin drinking wine from a bag, the closest they could get to the literary

illuminati of the thirties. Netta's voice brought him back from
those escapades.

"Is the Algonquin where you can order a martini with a
diamond in the bottom?"

"Yes, these days, so I've heard." He smiled at her lack of
erudition.

But she was a charming young woman, so earnest and—

He restrained himself from further analysis. He wasn't
feeling in top-notch shape yet.

Netta shoved the canoe to the water and got in the back. She
might as well be in the guide position this time. *That's the help
I'm getting. A hot tip on an unknown.* That was as close as she
was going to get to his manuscript, though she felt he wavered
just a little on the island, a thrilling moment. Maybe she did
have a future in publishing.

"I've got to pick a writer from the group too. They paid a
lot to come, after all."

He turned around to look at her directly saying, "And?
Who do you think?" His eyes were very blue and arresting,
giving her confidence in her hunch.

"Bea and Ruth are very clever. I'm going to ask them to send
the manuscript they told me about, a murder who-done-it.
They said it's based on a real case right here in the mountains."
In fact, they hinted there was more to the story than they had
revealed. Clearly, they liked her.

"And the ladies are very marketable. See, you're getting
the right instincts." He kept his paddle out of the water as
she dug in to glide them to the dock.

32

Pizza? It Can't Be Sunday!

O.T.'s REAPPEARANCE CHANGED THE RHYTHM of Sunday. Instead of a handful of guests remaining, Will figured he had almost a full house to feed. Lydia and Whit decided to stay over so he could drive his dad to Boston on Monday, and more writers delayed too. Will was rummaging in the freezer when Charlotte came into the kitchen. Just the open unit wasn't what made the air between them chilly.

"How about pizza?" she said closing the freezer.

"What? There's not enough cheese."

"No, let's just order pizza."

He looked at her. Never once in nineteen years had he served delivery pizza to lodge guests.

"Are you serious?" He pictured oily slices on a revolving warmer at the convenience store.

"Casual style, a pizza party with beer and soft drinks. You need a break from the kitchen. We need a break from—" She pointed out the screened door.

Will grimaced. His princess and O.T. were sitting amicably in lawn chairs. He hadn't told Charlotte that Bookman had come to the kitchen earlier offering to pay Alice's tuition.

"I've got it covered," he had said right off.

"How about grad school?"

190

The guy seemed anxious to do right and that was admirable, Will supposed. "We'll see when the time comes."

He'd pass this exchange along to Charlotte sometime. He felt her arms around him pulling them away from the door.

"I love you so much. You know that."

She sounded sincere, but he had to ask. "Wish you were living in Boston? You could have a different life with him." He kept his voice objective. He wanted her to be truthful.

"I'm North Country now, Will." Her body pressed along his could be a forecast for later, if he could let go of his resentment and believe her. "You can't get rid of me, Will, sorry. Besides, we have Alice. He doesn't." She gestured outside.

As if Alice had overheard them, she appeared.

"How about pizza tonight?"

"Your mom just suggested that, Allie. I don't know though."

"Get pizza from Rosco's. They even have Hawaiian and vegetarian."

He caught her let's-kid-dad look and made a face. "Hawaiian?"

"That's ham and pineapple."

"With cheese? Sounds—"

"Delicious." Alice grinned and went out the door saying, "Call them, Dad."

"This is going to cost a fortune." He looked at Charlotte.

"Did I hear Hawaiian pizza?" The dining room door swung inward bringing Lydia. "I'll charge dinner to the workshop. By the way, the writers and I have scored this week with the highest rating. You can count on more bookings from the seminar foundation. Maybe quilters next time. They would bring sewing machines but probably no surprises."

Will felt a nudge from her. "You're a prince, you know." She glanced over her shoulder to confirm Alice had left. "Charlotte, you were lucky making your early escape. O.T. sucked the life out of me. His partner in Boston must be made of stronger stuff, putting out a book every six months."

The women exchanged a long look that Will couldn't quite interpret. He shrugged. *Whatever. It was time to move on.*

"Okay, Char, call Rosco's. Better order beer too. And one of their chocolate cheesecakes that Allie likes."

Later, Will took in the conversation around the outdoor fire while the pizza, especially the Hawaiian, was passed around. He gathered Alice and Whit were exchanging life stories. He saw a likeness in their gestures and reminded himself these siblings could fill a niche in her future.

Lydia and O.T. sat a little apart without the graduate student at his elbow. She and the New York editor girl had formed an alliance and were in conference with the mystery writer ladies. "Synopsis . . . first chapters . . . Zenobia . . . New York meeting" drifted toward him. Charlotte's manuscript had been solicited that afternoon too. He tamped down qualms, keeping his resolution that this turn of events was not something to look at too closely—why her manuscript received the royal treatment—though he was certain of its excellence.

Will's musing ended when Bookman moved to sit nearby. Will saw he looked satisfyingly uncomfortable.

"Look, ah, Will, Luella and I would like to get to know Alice, and I'd like her to meet her sister, Maddie." He held out his phone. "Here she is, see?"

"Very sweet." Will wondered whether Charlotte had already seen the photo.

"Yes, she's the apple of my eye, though of course Alice is—"

"Yeah." *No need to spell it out.*

"So, what Maddie's mother and I thought was how about if for Thanksgiving—"

Focusing on the fire, he listened as Bookman babbled on about logistics. "Boston . . . airline ticket Wednesday . . . if Carly, sorry, your wife agrees."

Will's gut churned at his suggestion of taking Allie for Thanksgiving, the best holiday of the year in his opinion. A grand, deflective gesture was called for. He stood.

"Good idea for next year, man!" He offered Bookman a robust handshake and clap on the shoulder. "This year is Thanksgiving at Blackbird Lodge." He felt Charlotte sit up straight. "All your kids and significant others, and you, of course." He nodded toward O.T. "Everyone is invited."

Will could picture the scenes already. A twenty-pound turkey with his grandmother's chestnut stuffing—*what about grilled trout too*—sweet and white potatoes, and his mother's walnut pumpkin pie and Lady Baltimore cake. Maybe he could rent the mail boat from Sparky for a moonlit cruise, well, could be there'd be ice. *Even better.* Allie and her friends would lay out a skating rink. He began to figure the electricity cost of keeping the cabins heated so the water lines didn't freeze up.

🌿

Charlotte looked around as enthusiastic acceptances sounded after a brief silence. A Thanksgiving was in the works as old fashioned as a thousand-piece holiday puzzle! Leave it to Will to find a way to carry out a lodge tradition with a family larger than the Douglass clan and so much more complicated. *A blended family, how very modern. And woke!*

The tremor in Will's body told her his planning was underway. She had better speak up before the whole menu was solid.

"How about my spiced crab apples around the turkey? Of course, cranberry salads, jellied and raw, with oranges and walnuts."

When he said, "Sure, Char," to capitalize on his cooperation she added, "Brussels sprouts finished with toasted pine nuts, definitely." He flinched slightly at the Mediterranean garnish. She wound her arm around him observing O.T. talking to Alice, Whit, and Nate. It was a good time to take Will to the lodge alone. They had some intimate catching up to do.

☙

During the evening Alice had studied her two dads. Though of course she had known that DNA dad was out there somewhere, she hadn't thought he would turn up here or be a famous writer. Maybe it explained her way with words—a double genetic dose. She looked across the yard at this new dad. He was pleased to know about her, as far as she could tell. He was handsome in a way. She could see why women thought so, probably her friends would. But a reveal of that magnitude required much more thought.

When her brothers took a break from family stories, she said, "I think I'll just call your dad O.T. My mom and Lydia call him Otis."

"Thank God neither of us got named that," Nate said. "So close to odious!"

She felt free to laugh with them as they argued about who should have been the namesake until Whit settled it. "You're the oldest, you would be Otis." Nate made a dramatic gesture of a close call.

"Bookman is his pen name?" The name seemed awfully coincidental to her. She turned to Whit.

"Nope, he changed his surname after the divorce. We're stuck with Staszcyk, but you get Bookman, if you use it at all."

"He said he picked the name out of the phone book," Nate added. "But I bet his agent chose it."

A little more talk and then she went to her room. She felt worn out but motivated to make a notebook entry about the day and write a few lines of poetry. When she was done, she signed her work *Alice Elizabeth Bookman Adamsley*, with a flourish on the capital As.

☙

O.T. lay awake at midnight, alone. Lydia and he had come close to a liaison after some making out in the empty library, but ghosts and good judgment sent them to separate rooms upstairs.

He revisited his hospital musings of himself as the tragic hero. *But things didn't work out so well for those guys.* Romeo, there was a fervent lover, but his youthful judgment sucked. *I'm beyond that, thank God.* He continued his review.

Jay Gatsby, more modern, but Daisy Fay was unworthy of such love.

He contemplated his current state. *Not tragic, maybe heroic.* Yes, he should marry Luella, if she would have him. He would be just a family man now with his pack of kids. *Maybe I'll finish the book this year, maybe I won't.*

If he got an interview with NPR or, better yet, *Rolling Stone*, he'd acknowledge Charlotte's contributions to his best seller. He wasn't God's gift to his women. In fact, they were a gift to him, a cornerstone in his success. He needed to make sure Lydia understood his realization. He just had a feeling about the book, the memoir, she was writing—that he was in it.

———— • ————

33

— MONDAY —

Many Happy Returns . . .

Though seeming impossible to Charlotte, only the week before they had been waving to the departing Douglass Volvos. And now they were giving another group of cars the send-off, a tiny rental with Netta and Cinny, the Mustang with Lydia, Nate in his souped-up BMW, and the Lexus carrying O.T. driven by Whit.

Charlotte allowed herself some erudite ruminations as she made queenly waves. This family story wasn't finished. The narrative was still in draft, but major themes were settled on. *Would a classic trope emerge?* She considered the possibilities. Not a romance with her and Otis reunited, or a hero's journey—no one had changed significantly in many tests. *Well, Otis possibly a little.*

"It's only au revoir!" she said and sighed with drama, which resulted in Alice and Will putting their arms around her.

"I'm fine. I just thought of something amusing that's too hard to explain."

The story was more like a quest—her quest—and as protagonist she was lucky to discover she had been looking for the wrong things in coming up north. She had thought a writer needed unique geography and quirky characters, but stories were all around wherever you were, if you chose to observe with empathy. Her gaze took in the northern forest beyond the driveway, her husband Will, a hard-working, compassionate man, and Alice, their daughter already on her own journey.

✎

Sarah procrastinated in packing, not wanting to interfere with the goodbyes of the Adamsleys and others. Unpacking her suitcase upon arrival had been hard, and now packing up was equally distressing because the cabin had become a refuge. Leaving the North Country, she would have to face her empty house again. She took her bags to the lodge to be ready for her ride to Old Forge.

On an old-fashioned telephone stand in the front hall were reservation cards for return visits. She picked up one. Eight days ago she couldn't have imagined a return to Blackbird. She didn't have the first idea about the writing assignments as some of the others did and sharing a cabin had been challenging. Millicent would come in at all hours, sometimes quite boozy, and want to sit down and tell her everything as if in a sorority house. White Diamonds perfume from Millicent's cosmetics had seeped into her own clothes now. *Coming back was out.* Sarah put the card back down.

But what else did she have for plans, anyway? She would not be packing the car for the long-promised fall leaf tour with her husband. Myron had preferred golf to driving around, so her October sojourn had never materialized, and now he was dead. A small flicker of irritation made her pick up the card again and write in the first week in October. She would rent a cute car, ride up Whiteface Mountain in the ski gondola, visit the museum again, and lunch in Lake Placid to look for gifts for her grandchildren. Evenings in the library, she might write a love story, hers and Myron's or the tale of her grandmother's arranged marriage. "Very marketable," Netta and Cinny had assured her.

She filled in her address, phone, and so forth on the card. The final line was for choice of accommodation. Glancing up she saw Millicent heading out of their cabin with her enormous suitcase.

Oh, why not? Sarah made a checkmark next to Loon cabin for two.

———— • ————

Acknowledgment

THE CHARACTERS AND BLACKBIRD LODGE are works of fiction inspired by the Adirondack Park in New York and the historic Great Camps. I hope the novel represents the life of the New York's Adirondack Park as a whole, the intersection of history, preservation, and modern expectations.

Many thanks to three excellent editors who helped me. Kelly Finefrock is tireless in leaving notes and checking facts, as well as giving style help. Thank you, Christine Sullivan, for asking "Really?" about some plot details and making thoughtful suggestions. Finally, I'd like to pass along to other writers the excellent advice given me by author and editor Nancy Dafoe: "Don't rush the process!"

Thank you to my writing colleagues: Judy Troy, Lynn Olcott, Stephanie Medlock, Lisa Lee Petersen, and Susan Branch for reading drafts. I have great friends like Marie Greenhagen, Rosamund Potter, Sherry Moore, and Susan Nichols and others who suggested plot twists and listened to me dither. Thank you, also to 1106 Design for helping the book through the final gateways to publication.

I hope you enjoyed this book.
Would you do me a favor?

Like all authors, I rely on online reviews to encourage future sales. Your opinion is invaluable. Would you take a few moments now to share your assessment of my book at the review site of your choice? Your opinion will help the book marketplace become more transparent and useful to all.

Thank you very much!

Author and Illustrator Bios

AUTHOR JOYCE BURD HICKS grew up in Upstate New York. Her deep feelings for the mountains and Great Camps of the Adirondack Park began as a middle-school camper at Camp Huntington on Raquette Lake. The stories told there and subsequent visits inspired *Unexpected Guests at Blackbird Lodge*. A career move to a university in Indiana has given her a love of Chicago and midwestern life reflected in her novels *Escape from Assisted Living* and award-winning *One More Foxtrot*. She writes about domestic life and intricacies of marriage, particularly at gateways to new stages. She has performed at storytelling events in Chicago and belongs to writing groups. She is also a gardener and quilter. Find her at joycebhicks.com.

ILLUSTRATOR MELISSA WASHBURN grew up in the foothills of the Adirondack mountains, but has lived in the U.S. Midwest since 2005. An artist from the time she first picked up a crayon, she went through several other arts-adjacent careers before finding her niche in the illustration world. Her illustration work is endlessly inspired by things that run, fly, and grow. An avid hiker and birder, in 2019 she earned her Indiana Master Naturalist certification, and now serves on the Marketing and Communications committee of a local land trust. Her illustration work has appeared in numerous publications, including *Edible Michiana* and *Smithsonian* magazine, and she designed the mural of prairie flora and fauna on the kayak locker at the Dunes National Park in Gary, Indiana. She is also the author/illustrator of three books in the *Draw Like an Artist* series from Quarry Books. You can see more of her work at melissawashburn.com

———.———

Books by Joyce Hicks

Escape from Assisted Living

From the landmarks of Chicago to the wrong side of the law, Betty Miles's escape from senior living and her daughter's quest to bring her home tests everyone's assumptions about old age, family, and the kindness of secrets. Sharon D'Angelo thought it was a solid plan to move her widowed mother into a senior care facility. But after just three weeks, the octogenarian leaves via Amtrak when she learns there's a safe deposit box stashed away filled with who-knows-what. She has to find the truth, no matter the consequences.

Sharon is devastated to find Betty gone; a good daughter wouldn't lose her mother like this. She and her husband Vince trail after Betty, discovering along the way that their struggling marriage has its own secrets to confront and that a journey can change a family just as much as it can change an individual. (First in the Betty books.)

One More Foxtrot
First Prize 2018, Federation of Press Women
Finalist Indie Book Awards

The year after eighty-year-old Betty Miles's exit from senior living she's happy staying in Chicago with friend Eleanor. She's online dating, making new friends, and reconnecting with an old one. Her daughter, Sharon D'Angelo, is busy with her new dessert shop in Elkhart, Indiana. Good feelings between them may be short-lived after a stranger makes an astonishing claim. Will mother and daughter work through this mystery together? *Of course not.* They have kept upsetting truths secret their entire lives.

With her hands full—clients making moves on her husband Vince, her mother-in-law meddling in the desserts, and a visitor sleeping over—Sharon encourages Betty to stay away. Meanwhile, Betty's sleuthing family history, but her suspicions she keeps from Sharon. An accidental meeting in Chicago brings past transgressions to light: Will Betty and Sharon find that second chances bring just deserts?

Books by Melissa Washburn

 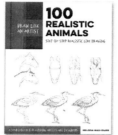 

100 Realistic Animals; 100 Flowers and Plants;
100 Birds, Butterflies, and Other Insects
by Melissa Washburn

Featuring 600+ sketches depicting a vast array of beautiful subjects, details, and more, the *Draw Like an Artist* series is a must-have visual reference for student artists, scientific illustrators, urban sketchers, and anyone seeking to improve their realistic drawing skills.

These contemporary, step-by-step guidebooks demonstrate fundamental art concepts like proportion, anatomy, and spatial relationships as you learn to draw a full range of nature subjects, all shown from a variety of perspectives. Each set of illustrations takes you from beginning sketch lines to a finished drawing.

Author Melissa Washburn is a skilled illustrator whose clear and elegant drawing style will make this a go-to sourcebook for years to come.

Made in United States
North Haven, CT
24 September 2023